Requiem
for a
Flower Child

Requiem for a Flower Child

A Jake Falcon Mystery

Warren Trest

NewSouth Books

Montgomery

NewSouth Books
105 S. Court Street
Montgomery, AL 36104

Copyright © 2015 by Warren Trest
All rights reserved under International and Pan-American Copyright
Conventions. Published in the United States by NewSouth Books, a
division of NewSouth, Inc., Montgomery, Alabama.

ISBN 978-1-60306-402-6 (paperback)
ISBN 978-1-60306-403-3 (ebook)

Printed in the United States of America

For Calder, Maya, and Naomi.
You light up our lives.

*Requiem
for a
Flower Child*

1

Jake Falcon's first case was over before it started. He was hired to find a daughter given up for adoption at birth only to have the client turn up dead the morning after he met with her. She had OD'd on pain killers. That's where the evidence pointed but Falcon wasn't buying it and neither was Chief Detective Earl Birdsong.

Falcon had taken the case as a favor to his pal Shooter. There was an aura of mystery about the client that intrigued him. Shooter described her as a middle-aged blues singer who failed to make it big at home but became a celebrity in Europe before being stricken with a terminal illness. Frail and unable to continue her career, she returned to Alabama to find the daughter she had never known and to make peace with the past.

She was christened Ophelia Jackson but was known by her stage name Maybelline, borrowed from Chuck Berry's 1950s' rock and roll classic. The few acquaintances she had in Montgomery knew her as Miss M, shortened to M by those closest to her. She kept strangers at arm's length for the most part and lived frugally in the projects out by the air base. She was under hospice care and Shooter came to know her through a paramedic at the base who did volunteer work in the community.

Falcon went with Shooter to M's apartment. A slender, attractive young woman came to the door and invited them in. Shooter introduced her as Jasmine, M's distant relative and part-time secretary. Looks were exchanged between Shooter and the young woman that made Falcon wonder if there was more to the relationship than met the eye. Jasmine served coffee and excused herself, saying she had to leave for the day.

M was propped up in bed with a large print Bible open beside her. On the bedside table were *The Collected Poems* of Langston Hughes, Ellison's *Invisible Man*, and *The Stranger* by Camus. Their incongruity was not lost on Falcon. It was apparent that M was seeking form and meaning in her life—but had she found them in the writings of others?

Falcon was drawn to the bedside of the intriguing chanteuse. On the wall were framed pictures at the peak of her career posing with entertainment icons Louis Armstrong, Nat King Cole, Fats Domino, Aretha Franklin, Etta James, Little Richard, celebrated French actor and entertainer Maurice Chevalier and a host of others. The cinnamon beauty of the woman in the pictures showed ever so faintly in M's pinched face and hands. Her hazel eyes with a hint of Irish green were now pools of worldly wisdom and faded passions. She was bright and articulate, just as saucy and street smart.

When she chose to tell her story Falcon pulled up a chair and sat by the bed to take notes. She began with a memory of being orphaned at an early age when her parents, who were professors at Tuskegee University, died in an automobile accident. A maiden aunt who lived in neighboring Russell County took her in, but was of meager means and could ill-afford another mouth to feed. M was on her own from her early teens.

She was singing with a small band that played in the clubs around Phenix City when she fell in love with a white soldier stationed across the river at Fort Benning, Georgia. His name was Johnny Gooden but he was known on the club circuit as Johnny B. Goode. He was a hot guitarist and played with the band on weekends. Their love risked more than malicious gossip for it was forbidden by Jim Crow statutes that were as bitter as the social mores that conceived them.

The young lovers moved in together but could not wed because Alabama and most Southern states had laws criminalizing interracial marriage. The day was over the horizon when the U.S. Supreme Court would strike down these discriminatory practices but such enlightened progress still had miles to go in the early 1950s. The lovers had to be doubly discreet in their relationship since miscegenation also was against the law.

Prying eyes are without modesty and word soon reached local authorities who threatened to bring charges against the couple. The commanding officer sought to resolve the problem by counseling the young soldier and placing him on restriction. When this didn't work—Johnny was caught slipping into town after dark—the commanding officer shipped him out to Korea where he was killed in action. The war was in its first year and Johnny was one of its early casualties. He died without knowing M was carrying his child.

M learned of Johnny's death from another soldier who was a former member of the band. Her heart was broken. Pulling herself together she continued to sing with the band and worked at odd jobs to try and make ends meet. Johnny had told her nothing about his family and she was taken by surprise when a man showed up on her doorstep claiming to be an attorney representing the Gooden family. He was from Montgomery and gave his name as Sam Reuben. M invited him in only to be rendered more helpless and despondent by what he had to say.

Reuben was small of stature and flashily dressed with slicked-back hair, a pencil-thin mustache, a slight lisp and what struck M as an affected nasal drawl. He told M that the Gooden family had authorized him to pay her medical expenses and reward her handsomely if she agreed to put the baby up for adoption and leave the state. M declined the offer and asked to meet with the family. That was not going to happen, Reuben assured her. He departed in a huff, leaving M shaken by a strident riposte. "You're making a big mistake, Missy. You surely are."

Soon after Reuben's visit a deputy sheriff came to the apartment asking questions and intimating that M might be arrested for breaking the law. Although Reuben did not return to her door, for days on end it seemed that either he or the deputy popped up wherever she went, even showing up at clubs where she and the band were billed. Then Reuben dropped out of sight until she was in the hospital about to deliver her baby. M spotted him in the anteroom consulting with the doctor when the nurse came in to administer the anesthetic.

When M came out from under the anesthetic her baby, a daughter, had been taken away and she had purportedly signed a statement consenting to adoption of the child by foster parents. She was told that the adoption was legally witnessed and notarized. She was not allowed to see her newborn child and when she protested the doctor ordered nurses to keep her sedated the remainder of her stay in the hospital.

After she was released from the hospital the distraught young mother was mentally and emotionally drained. She was without resources and didn't know where to turn. Desperate calls to the doctor's office and the hospital were not returned. Then the sheriff's deputy showed back up with a restraining order and threatened that if she continued to harass the doctor and hospital staff she would be put in jail and the county would take the baby from her anyway.

The ubiquitous Sam Reuben arrived on the heels of the deputy's visit with another offer of assistance he said she couldn't refuse. He had a wad of small bills, a Greyhound bus ticket to New Orleans, and a letter of introduction for the young singer to the manager of a popular nightclub on Bourbon Street. "I'd take this most generous offer if I was you, Missy. There won't be another." Alone and afraid M had packed her few belongings and took the bus to the Big Easy.

Telling her story had exhausted M and she abruptly stopped, coughed and spit blood into a small receptacle beside the bed. Shooter went to the kitchen and brought her a glass of water. She sipped from the glass and coughed again. Did she want to continue at a later time, Falcon asked? She apologized and waved him off. No, she just needed to rest a moment. She thought it was important for Falcon to know what happened when she returned from Europe and would finish telling the story while it was fresh in her thoughts. She wanted to bring him up to date so he could start looking for her daughter right away.

2

M's youth was more present for her than were current events. A French lover once said to her, earnestly if breathlessly, that "we lift the veil from the endless summers of our youth to see who we really are. They have placed a lien on our souls that last forever while the long winters of our discontent are little more than driftwood tossed upon the ocean currents or straws in the wind." Falcon wondered if M had relived the defining moments of her life so often they were as much a part of the healing as her evening devotions? He listened patiently as she attempted to make sense of what had occurred since her return from Europe.

She had been wary of returning to Phenix City and came to Montgomery instead believing that the state capital offered opportunities more favorable for locating her daughter. Montgomery was the hub of the Civil Rights Movement and she thought people there would be more receptive to her quest. She leased an apartment in Montgomery and before becoming too infirm did charity work while undertaking the search for her daughter. The search proved more elusive than she ever imagined.

Early on she checked with the Department of Public Health and was told there was no record of anyone with her name having given birth to a child during the 1950s in Phenix City or anywhere else in Alabama. How could that be? The clerk assured her there was no record of birth on file and that was the end of it.

M's hopes now rested with the hospital in Phenix City, the doctor who delivered her baby, and perhaps the threatening sheriff's deputy or the self-styled middle man Sam Reuben if that truly was his name and if he still had an office in Montgomery. Reuben's name was not in the Yellow Pages but she tracked him down eventually in a rundown part of town and made an appointment to see him.

The years had taken their toll. Reuben before was just small, now bent and thin as a stick. He had fallen on hard times but was still nattily dressed. At first he couldn't place M but a glimmer of recognition showed when she revealed her purpose in being there. His face reddened and he reached in his back pocket for a handkerchief to wipe the beads of sweat from his brow. "I don't know what your game is madam. I never saw you before and I have no earthly idea what you are talking about." He spoke with false conviction but the darting eyes gave him away.

Reuben showed her out. "We live in a different world today," M reminded him and promised she would be back. Several days later she returned with a young lawyer acquaintance of Jasmine's to confront Reuben and found the office closed. The entrance was roped off and men in dark suits were hauling the office files away. They were obviously federal agents. At this point the nervous young lawyer thought it might be better for M to retain someone in Phenix City to look into the matter and represent her.

M had Jasmine drive her to Phenix City where the landscape was altered dramatically from the day she left town, her spirit broken and forlorn, on the back seat of a Greyhound bus—and for her it was a lifetime ago. The seedy clubs and juke joints that once gave the wicked city its name had given way to urban sprawl. Nothing looked the same.

The old clubs where the band once played were gone and the apartment complex where she and Johnny consummated their love for each other had been razed. The hospital was still there. It had expanded at one point and now seemed to be in decline—but yet a ghostly shell of brick and mortar. Those among the former doctors and nursing staff who were still living had all retired or moved away. The deputy sheriff who threatened her had been found guilty of a hired killing and died in prison.

As a last resort M hired a private detective in Phenix City named Mike Skinner who boasted prophetically that he would get to the truth for her or die trying. Weeks passed and she heard nothing from Skinner. An answering service took her calls until the connection went dead and the minty voice on the other end had in its place a tinny drone. That's when Falcon and Shooter entered the picture. M confided to Shooter about the seemingly insurmountable obstacles she encountered and Shooter leaned on his friend Falcon for help.

M ended her story on that note. She had another coughing spell, but without spitting blood. A faint sigh signaled to her guests that she had talked herself out and would have to rest. "That's the gist of it, Colonel Falcon. Come back tomorrow and Jasmine will write a check for your retainer." As they rose to leave she brushed aside Shooter's concerns that someone needed to be there to look after her. Jasmine would return the following afternoon and a person from hospice care came around to check on her through the day.

As they left the apartment Falcon shook off an overpowering sense of dread—eerily similar to ones he experienced before taking off for strikes against the heavily defended Ho Chi Minh Trail in Laos. The old hands ragged him that it was a sure sign either his or another fighter pilot's date with the reaper had come. There was no truth in the saying—the foreboding struck before every mission regardless of whether any unit aircraft were lost or not. Shooter didn't seem to notice the change in Falcon's mood.

Arriving back at the Piedmont Hotel, Shooter peeled off to open the bar while Falcon went to his room to mull over what M had told them. If he was going to find the missing daughter he would first have to prove she existed. Assuming that M was telling the whole truth, and he had no reason to doubt her, the lack of a birth certificate or other corroborating evidence raised questions. Was it shoddy records keeping by Public Health officials or was a more sinister plot at play? Was the simple truth hidden in the tangled web of Phenix City's notorious past?

Falcon was familiar with the history of racial injustice in the South and in the back of his mind were fragments he had picked up about Phenix City corruption before it was cleaned up—bits and pieces of the past that tied corrupt public officials to about every conceivable criminal enterprise including a so-called baby mill and adoption racket. Without this background to glue the pieces together M's story might not hold water or at least would be exceedingly difficult to prove.

Someone Falcon wanted to consult about Phenix City's past was Major George Thunder, a Special Forces officer he had known in Vietnam who was now assigned to Army criminal investigations at Fort Benning, Georgia. Major Thunder was half Cherokee and was born and raised in the local area. If there was anyone among Falcon's acquaintances who knew where the skeletons were buried across the Chattahoochee River from Fort Benning it would be George Thunder.

Before Falcon had a chance to speak with Thunder, however, he found himself in Chief Detective Earl Birdsong's office explaining what he and Shooter were doing in M's apartment the evening prior to her death. Neighbors had reported seeing two suspicious men matching their descriptions leaving the dead woman's apartment and Birdsong had dispatched a patrol car to bring Falcon in for questioning.

Falcon had bonded with M and found her death hard to reconcile with what she had told him. The shock he now felt was betrayed by his relaxed image, which was in sharp contrast with the ramrod figure his questioner portrayed looking down on him from behind an oversized desk. Under Birdsong's steady gaze Falcon remained expressionless. His lanky frame settled deeper into the cushioned chair. People acquainted with the two men were accustomed to the casual play between them. They were friendly rivals, having worked reciprocal cases when Falcon was assigned to special investigations at Maxwell Field.

They were two sides of a coin: Jake Falcon, Air Force Academy grad, smooth and edgy, a little laid back, drifting toward Nirvana, a burned out fighter pilot who went cross-wise to his general-officer father by leaving the military early; Earl Birdsong, a self-made man, rough around the edges, gruff and burly, playing by the book and on his way up in the Capital City's police department. One a divorcee with a limited independent income, his own plane, a classic Corvette convertible, and a hotel room to call home; the other a nine-to-five family man, mortgaged to the hilt with two cars and a house in the suburbs, living on a weekly allowance, working through lunch to pinch pennies; both Vietnam Vets and the unlikeliest of friends.

Their verbal jousting aside—Falcon found it preposterous that he and Shooter would be treated with suspicion in the case—Birdsong accepted Falcon's explanation of what he and Shooter were doing at the dead woman's apartment. He shared Falcon's hunch about foul play being involved and a coroner's report would back them up. Bruises and lacerations on M's face, upper body, and inside her mouth served as convincing evidence that she was force fed the bottle of painkillers while being strangled. But the question remained, why would anyone want to murder a dying woman? That's what Birdsong and Falcon, each in his own way, intended to find out.

3

Falcon returned with one of Birdsong's detectives to M's apartment to look for additional evidence. The crime scene was taped off and, at Falcon's request, Jasmine was allowed to enter the apartment and she met them at the door. There were no signs of forced entry or the muted struggle that surely had taken place. M left the door unlocked and anyone could have waltzed right in. She would have been too weak to fight off an intruder for long. She had no enemies that Jasmine knew about. No valuables were missing.

After he and Shooter departed the previous evening M had arranged neat stacks of papers and photographs on the floor beside the bed. They had not been disturbed even by the men who had taken her body to the morgue. Falcon rummaged through the stacks and retrieved a few items he thought might be useful. One was a faded photograph of a young three-striper in uniform he took to be M's true love Johnny Gooden. The photograph was wrapped in tissue and kept inside a manila envelope. Flipping through an album of pictures he saw that one was missing. Jasmine thought M might have removed the picture or it could have fallen out.

The contrast in book titles on the bedside table still had Falcon's interest. Jasmine explained that M had been an avid reader and was self-taught. She spoke French fluently and was a patron of the arts. Falcon leafed through The Stranger. M had underlined a passage which described the protagonist Meursault, a prisoner on trial for murder, facing up to the reality that the people in the courtroom loathed him. Another marked passage referenced Meursault's denial of belief in an afterlife. Their grim finality seemed out of character and caused Falcon to brush aside a dark thought that perhaps M had been capable of taking her own life.

Over the weekend Falcon went with Shooter to M's funeral. Only a handful of mourners were there. Shooter said M would have wanted it that way. She had a small circle of admirers but shunned publicity since her return. During the little time she had left the only people M had the energy to help were children's causes and society's throwaways who led lives of quiet desperation in homeless shelters or behind bars. As her health deteriorated she had to drop these outside activities altogether. Members of her favorite charities were noticeably absent. Shooter was not surprised. They were not named in M's will and deceased donors don't write checks.

Falcon searched the faces of the mourners, wondering if there was a killer among them. Three of the mourners looked out of place. In an aside Falcon whispered his suspicions to Shooter who suppressed a smile. One of the mourners in question was a city council member representing M's district, another the minister who was there to deliver the eulogy and the third was one of Birdsong's undercover detectives sent there there to size up the others in attendance including Falcon and Shooter.

When the councilman left before the service was over Shooter wondered aloud had the big man been intimidated by the small size of the crowd. The minister also departed after delivering the eulogy and paying his respects to Jasmine, the only family member there. A small Salvation Army band played New Orleans funeral jazz as they lowered the casket into the ground. "Oh, she's smiling now," Shooter said.

On the drive back from the cemetery Falcon corrected him. "I don't think so. She's not smiling I mean, not until her killer is brought to justice and her daughter is found." Shooter could tell from the jutting jaw and the tone of his voice that Falcon was still in the game. He no longer had a client or a case but he had the scent and he felt an obligation. Only the game had taken a far more ominous turn with M's murder and nothing about the murder made any sense. But then murder rarely does.

4

Now that he was in the hunt Falcon would leave no stone unturned in finding M's killer and her long-lost daughter. He wanted to delve into Sam Reuben's files but couldn't gain access without breaking and entering and he wasn't about to take on the feds. The doors to the Department of Public Health were open and he went there to double-check the accuracy of the missing birth certificate. The clerk assured him that the information given to M was correct. There was no record of her having given birth to a child in Alabama.

When Falcon left the building a woman followed him out and caught up with him. She overheard his conversation with the desk clerk and thought she might have information of interest. She introduced herself as a Public Health employee named Susan who used to be assigned to the front desk. They went across the street to a small café where they could talk privately.

Susan read in the Montgomery Advertiser about the murder and recognized the victim as the woman who had come to the Public Health office concerning her daughter's birth certificate. Susan had been promoted to a supervisory position but came out of her office to see what the commotion was about and found the woman distraught. The woman left before Susan could intervene. She later reviewed the report of complaint filed by the desk clerk and it reminded her of a similar occurrence a few years back.

In the earlier incident a young woman of mixed race had come to the front desk seeking a record of her birth and information concerning her natural parents. No record was found. At that time she believed the young woman had been misinformed about the facts surrounding her birth, but now she wondered. She tried to locate the older woman who fit M's description to give her this information but no one could recall her name or where she lived. The woman had filled out a form but in the commotion she left taking the form with her. She had neglected to sign the desk register.

Susan described the younger inquirer from a few years back as a beautiful innocent. She was barefoot, wore a long flowing skirt and a gypsy blouse, hippie-style, silky and braless. A male companion in a Nehru jacket and bell bottoms was perhaps a few years older, but Susan had been so entranced with the young woman's appearance she paid him little attention. She followed them to the door when they left and saw them drive away in a psychedelic Volkswagen bus. There could have been other young people inside the bus. She wasn't sure.

Falcon knew the Vegas odds but the young woman Susan described could be M's long lost daughter. He gave Susan his card and she promised to let him know if she recalled more about the incident involving the mysterious flower child or if anyone else came looking for her. She believed flower child was what the hippie girls called themselves. Could be she read it in Cosmopolitan or Rolling Stone.

From there Falcon drove over to Fort Benning and met Major Thunder outside the main gate at a place called the Hamburger Heaven, a greasy spoon cafe known for its mouth-watering burgers and warm beer flat as rainwater. He had given a brief account of M's story over the phone and knew George Thunder would go to any lengths to help. He couldn't count the times when North Vietnamese regulars had Thunder's Special Forces penned down in Laos and jet fighters from Falcon's unit zoomed in to even the odds. The gunfighters were just doing their job but men like George Thunder never forget.

M's chronicle of racial injustice brought back memories of Thunder's own youthful misadventures growing up on an Army base across the river from Sin City. His father was a career Army officer with rows of fruit salad on his uniform but that cut no ice with the local community where corruption was rampant and bigotry against people of color was law. George Thunder was not familiar with M's personal circumstances but knew the baby rackets had flourished as part of the widespread corruption in Sin City before a crooked deputy sheriff gunned down State Attorney General-elect Albert Patterson on a hot, humid summer night in 1954.

Sixty-three year old Albert Patterson, former state senator and severely wounded veteran of World War I, had campaigned for Attorney General on a pledge to clean out the mob and dirty politicians. His brutal murder sparked a public outcry that forced state officials to finish the cleanup he started. His eldest son John was elected to replace his father as Attorney General and he played a lead role in cleaning up Phenix City and making sure the criminals and crooked politicians did not fall back into their old ways.

John Patterson's crime-fighting image propelled the political novice into the Governor's mansion four years later. In 1958 the 38-year-old Attorney General defeated a formidable slate of gubernatorial hopefuls including George Wallace to become Alabama's youngest elected governor. In the course of Alabama political history this made John Patterson the only candidate to ever defeat George Wallace in a gubernatorial race.

George Thunder and his family were not Alabama voters but they were loyal Patterson supporters. Thunder's father had served with John Patterson in the North African and Italian campaigns in World War II and they had become fast friends. When John finished Law School on the GI Bill and joined his father's practice in Phenix City they were the Thunder family's attorneys. The family had the highest respect for John Patterson and his father and they were devastated when Albert Patterson was murdered.

Major Thunder recalled that one of the last cases John Patterson and his father tried together involved an unwed mother whose situation was eerily similar to what Falcon told him about M being coerced into giving her daughter up for adoption. He didn't remember the details of the other case—to the best of his memory it was known as the unwed mother case—but he suggested Falcon explore the similarities with former Governor John Patterson.

George Thunder had taken the liberty of setting up a meeting with the former governor. "He and his law partner have offices in the Bell Building in Montgomery. It's rumored that he may be next in line for an appointment to the State Court of Criminal Appeals when there's a vacancy. You two will get along fine. He's an interesting fellow. And he's lived in interesting times. He's expecting your call."

Thunder gave Falcon the little information he had on the once thriving black market adoption rackets. In the 1940s-50s the rackets had reached across state lines in the Deep South, the Midwest, and along the Eastern Seaboard into Washington, D.C. In November 1955 a Senate Subcommittee held hearings into juvenile delinquency and the effects of the widespread practice of selling babies. Senator Estes Kefauver of Tennessee, a state where a notorious baby mill had been exposed, chaired the hearings and Attorney General John Patterson of Alabama was a key witness.

Some witnesses rationalized that the adoption mills found loving homes for infants who might otherwise be orphaned but the fact remained that the widespread practice of selling babies was more about profit than social welfare. Baby brokers, some with ties to the mob, handled many of the illegal adoptions and worked hand-in-hand with corrupt local and state officials. Big-time political hacks were involved. In the Phenix City area prostitutes and B-girls were part of the rackets. Many an unsuspecting GI fathered offspring and never knew it. The babies were sold at a heavenly price. As a rule there was no screening of adoptive parents. All they needed was cash on delivery and a little extra to grease a greedy public servant's palm. The Kefauver report noted that in one egregious case, a dangerous fugitive with a long criminal record was allowed to adopt one of the infants.

Thunder had little to offer concerning M's lover Johnny Gooden. There were hundreds of stories about recalcitrant soldiers or repeat offenders being shipped out to remote assignments either as a form of discipline or to keep them out of trouble. He would have someone check the records for Falcon and get back to him on it. The names of the commanding officers for that period were readily available, as were the records for war casualties, burials, etc. This should lead to Johnny Gooden's parents, to where he was buried, and maybe even to who had adopted M's daughter.

One bit of unsettling information had to do with the private detective M hired in Phenix City but never heard from again. When Falcon brought up the name Mike Skinner he got an inquisitive look from George Thunder. Falcon hadn't seen the morning paper which headlined a story about Skinner's body being found in the driver's seat of his Ford Mustang at the bottom of the Chattahoochee River.

The mangled Mustang with Skinner's corpse at the wheel had been there for several days. He had enough booze in his veins to embalm a platoon. According to the article in the Columbus Ledger foul play was not suspected in Skinner's death but the news added to the mystery surrounding M's murder and the search for her daughter.

George Thunder had to attend a staff meeting and Falcon was late for an appointment with Chief Detective Birdsong. As they walked out of the Hamburger Heaven toward the parking lot, Thunder abruptly broke stride and charged over to a mud-splattered truck with oversized tires and a camouflage paint job. What caught Thunder's eye was a child's Aunt Jemima doll with a noose tied around its neck hanging from the truck's grill. Thunder cut the doll loose and tossed it in the truck's bed. "Must have followed you here," he said to Falcon. "That piece of trash would never make it past the gate guard at Benning."

On the drive back to Montgomery, Falcon spotted a truck in his rear-view mirror similar to the one in the café parking lot. He slowed to get a closer look and when he did, the truck dropped back and kept its distance. He shrugged it off when the truck turned onto a side road leading to Tuskegee, only to sit up and take notice when it reappeared minutes later on the highway behind him.

Playing musical chairs on the open road was not his form of entertainment. He couldn't be sure whether the driver was tailing him or making deliveries when the truck repeated the turn-off maneuver a couple of miles down the highway. The truck made a final exit as they approached the city limits and the flashing blue lights of a police cruiser appeared out of nowhere, cut in front of Falcon and instead of pulling him over led the way to Earl Birdsong's office.

Falcon got the message that he was late for the appointment with Earl but having a patrol car with flashing blue lights escort him in was a bit extreme. Or was this just Earl's way of letting him know that his movements were on the radar screen and reminding him who was in charge of investigating M's murder? As long as Falcon stayed in the game he was playing in Earl's ballpark, like it or not. He didn't want to get under Earl's skin but neither did he want the boys in blue watching his every move. They would have to find common ground.

5

Before Falcon could raise the issue of the police escort Birdsong dropped a bombshell. His investigators had fingered Jasmine as a person of interest in M's murder and he wanted Falcon to know they were bringing her in for questioning. "The sheriff in Dallas County picked her up this morning. They're on their way here from Selma as we speak." Jasmine had moved in with relatives in Selma temporarily because she was afraid to stay in the Montgomery apartment alone.

"You can't be serious."

"Is my name Earl?"

"This is unbelievable!"

"Believe this," Earl said and pushed a sheaf of papers across the desk. On top was a copy of M's will. She had recently changed her will leaving everything to her daughter. If the daughter didn't turn up, then Jasmine was the presumptive heir and stood to inherit a small fortune. The clincher according to Earl—his investigators were suspicious that the young lawyer who drew up the will was Jasmine's boyfriend and she had recommended him to M.

"You don't hold someone for murder based on suspicions."

"We're not holding her. We're bringing her in for questioning. There's more. We'll get enough on her to convene a grand jury."

"They won't indict."

"How do you figure?"

Falcon said it made no sense for Jasmine to have committed the murder. No one knew better than she that M was on her death bed and was not long for this world.

Birdsong said the answer to that was simple. She knew M was going to hire Jake to find the daughter and had to move fast.

"You forget that Jasmine's lawyer friend was the one who suggested M go to Phenix City and hire another lawyer or private investigator."

"What makes you think that wasn't just to throw us off. That private eye could've been killed to shut him up." Earl had picked up on the police wire that the PI Mike Skinner's body had been found swimming with the fish in the Chattahoochee.

"What about me? I'm still walking around on two good legs."

"You could be next."

How can you argue with logic like that? Earl had closed the door on common ground and Falcon wanted no part of it. He didn't want to be there when they brought Jasmine in or she might think he had a hand in her arrest. He walked out before the conversation ended and headed to the Piedmont. Shooter would be climbing the wall by now.

6

Former Governor John Patterson was not the elderly barrister Falcon expected to meet when the secretary ushered him into her boss's office. He looked surprisingly young—trim, ruggedly handsome with firm jaw, slightly receding hairline, bushy eyebrows without a hint of gray, and a relaxed Southerner's charm that made folks feel right at home. Coming of age in the Great Depression, serving in two wars, taking up his father's fight against crime and corruption, and a four year term as Alabama's youngest elected Governor had ingrained in him the equanimity and self-confidence for taking on major crises or business as usual.

Falcon found him to be congenial, someone who enjoyed meaningful conversation but did not engage in small talk. An hourglass at his fingertips was a novel way of staying on schedule while keeping faith with history and tradition. "I've been expecting you, Colonel. George Thunder said you were over at the fort stirring up the ashes of old wars and injustices. Pull up a chair and sit a spell. You're up first. Fire both barrels."

Patterson turned on a tape recorder and sat back to listen. Falcon drew a deep breath and delivered a straightforward, military style briefing of what he had learned thus far about M's murder and the futile search for her daughter. When Falcon finished briefing him Patterson confirmed George Thunder's observation that M's abuse at the hands of the baby sellers in Phenix City had parallels to the unwed mother case he and his father tried during that same period. Copies of the March 1955 Alabama Supreme Court summary of the case, *Griggs v. Barnes* [262 Ala. 1955] and the 1955 Kefauver

Committee report were on the desktop to refresh his memory.

Then it was Falcon's turn to listen. Patterson kept the recorder running to tape his own comments. In 1951, when the Army recalled him to active duty and he served in Europe, his father was retained as the attorney for a teenage mother whose newborn child, a baby boy, had been taken from her and given to foster parents. A mirror of M's experience without the interracial aspects, the unwed mother purportedly signed an agreement consenting to the adoption while still under the influence of an anesthetic at the hospital. Upon being released from the hospital she wanted to know where her baby was and nobody would tell her. From that point she had tried continuously to get her baby back.

Patterson's father, representing the teenage mother, filed a petition for habeas corpus which was tried in the Circuit Court of Russell County. She lost her case in the lower court and it was appealed to the Alabama Supreme Court. The high court ruled in favor of the natural mother but the local sheriff failed to deliver the child as ordered and the foster parents appealed the ruling. The case was still pending in the summer of 1954 when Albert Patterson was murdered. John Patterson took over the case and the Supreme Court upheld the earlier ruling to turn the child back to the natural mother.

The higher court's decision came when Phenix City was under martial law and the National Guard was called in to restore law and order. The cleanup of the city exposed that the criminal syndicate had eaten its way into the very fabric of life in Phenix City with political influence reaching into the halls of the State Capital. It was out of this situation that the baby-adoption ring had grown and flourished. As part of the cleanup the former sheriff and other corrupt public officials who had done the syndicate's bidding were removed from office. After the higher court denied the appeal a new sheriff delivered the child to the natural mother.

This was the first time that the natural mother had seen the child since its birth, Patterson said, and the child by this time was nearly 4 years old. He remembered it being a very sad thing to take the child at that age, but the natural mother was entitled under the law. She was not at fault in the long period of time that passed, he said, because she tried diligently, from the very beginning, to get custody of her child, and it was through the self-serving efforts of others that she was unable to do so.

The natural mother had married in the interim and claimed she had been threatened and intimidated on numerous occasions before the court's reversal and afterward. The notoriety of her case influenced a National Guard investigation into other adoption cases. The investigation revealed that a pattern of fraudulent activity existed and the adoption rackets were operating in a way designed to get around the Alabama adoption laws.

Patterson did not find it surprising that M had been unable to find a birth certificate for her daughter in her name or the father's name. In the case he and his father tried the baby boy was not registered in the hospital under the birth mother's name but under the names of the foster parents and the address given was that of the foster parents. The birth certificate had been issued fraudulently in their names. It was logical to suspect that something similar had occurred in M's situation—find out who adopted M's daughter and the birth certificate would likely turn up.

In M's situation the involvement of a shady character like Sam Reuben muddied the waters. "I don't believe in coincidences," Patterson said. "We have to proceed on the logical assumption that Reuben's disappearance is connected in some way to M's death and that of the private detective they found at the bottom of the Chattahoochee. A circle of violence seems to be in play. M's murder may be the centrifugal force but does it end with her? Looks like we have to go down that winding road and see where it takes us."

Another side to the mystery he found puzzling was the Gooden family connection. The father of M's child was from somewhere in Alabama, or so Sam Reuben implied when he first contacted her, but the family name was not common to the local area. There was a prominent, well-established family by that name in Catawba County north of the Capital City, Patterson said, but there was no evidence they were the family involved. The patriarch of the clan, old man Luther, and his wife Tallulah died in a fire awhile back and were buried on the estate. Patterson didn't know Luther and Tallulah. They didn't support him for governor and he was never invited on their land.

The Goodens owned half the county, it was said, and they were very clannish folks. They lived way back in the woods with a big mansion on the hill. Patterson recalled driving past the estate when he was campaigning for governor. All that was visible from the road were miles of woods, barbed wire fences, and no-trespassing signs. "They say a fellow can walk from sunset to sundown without leaving their property. The only folks who stepped on every foot of land up there, I'm told, wore moccasins. And that was before Alabama became a State."

Patterson said he would rummage around and see what he could come up with about Johnny Gooden's family and the missing broker Sam Reuben. Falcon's next stop was the State Archives to go through back issues of the Catawba County Clarion to see what had been printed about the Goodens. If they were the right family the story about their son being killed in Korea would be in the papers.

Falcon raised the issue of Jasmine's incarceration. Neither he nor Shooter had been allowed to visit her in jail. Patterson said he would take care of the matter. "They either charge the young woman or let her go. We'll put a stop to this before the sun goes down."

When Falcon took out his checkbook Patterson waved him off. "George Thunder told me you were flying this mission all on your own. Tell you what, I teach a night class at Troy University. You register for the class and we'll both get something out of it." Falcon didn't protest. Looking around the Bell Building he figured he couldn't afford the price anyway.

While the secretary made a copy of the tape Patterson reached in his desk drawer and took out a fifth of Hennessy cognac and two crystal snifters. "Let's have a spot or two to toast our new relationship, Colonel. There are times when my law partner and I need a top investigator and I have a feeling you're going to require someone to interpret the law for you now and then."

Patterson was pensive as they tipped the glasses. "If that young mother had only known to go to my father for help back then, he would have taken her case pro bono, which he often did, and fate might have dealt her a better hand. Why does the darker realm of society always prey on the young and helpless, Colonel? Perhaps you and I have a chance to make it up to her before we're done with this case."

7

The Catawba County Clarion's masthead claimed to cover the news like the morning dew, but Falcon found surprisingly little about the county's most prominent family in back issues of the paper. A closer look at the masthead revealed a likely explanation: Luther and Tallulah Gooden were the owners and publishers.

A news story that grabbed Falcon's attention was the Clarion's coverage of a memorial service that took up the whole front page of an early Fifties edition of the paper. He thought he'd stumbled on the Holy Grail upon reading that Luther and Tallulah's only son, Johnny Gooden, had been killed in Korea. Only the story when read in its entirety raised as many questions as it did answers.

Johnny Gooden had been buried with full military honors and was laid to rest in a private cemetery on the family estate. There was no mention of M or a daughter but a son Johnny Gooden Jr. was listed among surviving family members. This was the first Falcon heard about Johnny Gooden having a son. The name of the son's mother was left out of the article.

There were no recent copies of the Clarion on microfilm at the State Archives leading Falcon to believe the paper had gone under after Luther and Tallulah's deaths. The desk clerk helped him identify newspapers from adjacent counties and he found stories about Luther and Tallulah dying in a fiery explosion when their mansion went up in flames and burned to the ground. The article made reference to other possible deaths in the fire but did not identify the victims.

In a recent edition of one paper he read that complaints had been made by residents of neighboring counties concerning gunfire and loud explosions coming from the estate. There were also reports of heavy traffic going in and out of the property. The paper cited the existence of an exotic private hunting club and extensive mining operations to account for the unusual amount of activity in and around the estate and the sporadic gunfire and loud explosions reported by passersby and residents in surrounding areas.

Before leaving the Archives he looked at Montgomery Advertiser accounts of Sam Reuben's disappearance. That was a square he had to fill but the newspaper stories provided no clue to what happened to Reuben or to his whereabouts. Reuben left the office one morning without telling his secretary where he was going and never returned. No one came forward with credible information. Reuben was a loner and had no immediate family so far as anyone knew. The State had placed his estate in escrow pending the feds resolution of the case. And the feds weren't talking.

On the way out Falcon stopped at the front desk and called Shooter to see if he'd heard from Jasmine. Good news! Shooter was leaving now to pick her up and take her back to Selma. Both men were impressed at how quickly the former governor had secured her release. Earl Birdsong's feathers were ruffled but he would get over it.

Falcon went from the Archives over to the Convention Center where a gun show was in progress. The old Army 45 was a relic and Falcon found it cumbersome to carry. He was looking for a lighter weapon. He had his license to carry with him and ended up at a booth where he purchased a Beretta with just the right balance and fit nicely on the hip or under the shoulder.

Exiting the Convention Center he was blinded by the noonday sun. He headed across to where the convertible was parked and pulled up short. Shading his eyes he spotted a camouflage truck parked next to the convertible. It looked like the one that followed him back from Phenix City but he couldn't be certain until he saw a black-face doll hanging on a noose from the front of the vehicle. An altercation had broken out between the driver of the truck and an airman in khakis.

Before blows could be exchanged a police cruiser pulled up and a city policeman got out and stepped in between the two men. Falcon was close enough to hear the conversation. The altercation started when the airman noticed the black-face doll hanging on the truck's grill and demanded that the driver remove it. The policeman confiscated the doll and issued the driver a summons for disturbing the peace. Then he shook the airman's hand and gave him a lift to his destination.

Falcon wrote down the truck's license number as it pulled out of the parking lot and roared up the street. The incident lost some of its edginess when he spotted a front plate portraying the doddering figure of a Rebel soldier carrying a Confederate flag and below it the dim-witted tee-shirt phrase, "Forget, Hell!" But he wouldn't soon forget the skinny, pony-tailed driver with the angry, bloodshot eyes and corn-colored wisp of a goatee.

He removed a flyer attached behind the convertible's windshield and tossed it on the floorboard. The message on the flyer was more disturbing than the cornball humor on the truck's front plate. It bore a picture of a fierce, uniformed Nathan Bedford Forrest wielding a saber on horseback and the message "Take Our Country Back!" The message was attributed to a group calling itself the New Freedom Brigade.

He dropped by police headquarters to discuss the flyer with Earl Birdsong. Neither man brought up the subject of Earl's detectives having to release Jasmine. Earl was still sulking. He had never heard of the New Freedom Brigade and it was not on any list of banned or subversive organizations that crossed his desk. He dismissed the flyer as a childish prank.

Falcon assured him it was no prank and told him about the incident in the Convention Center parking lot. The driver of the truck appeared to be the same one who earlier had tailed him to Fort Benning and back. Earl called the traffic division and got the driver's name and information from the incident report which the policeman had just finished writing up.

The offender's name was Billy Joe Sparrow, a younger brother to Sheriff Amos Sparrow in Catawba County. The truck was registered to the sheriff's department there. "I'd leave it alone if I was you. That is unless you feel harassed again or something worse happens." That crowd, Earl said, was nobody to mess with, particularly Sheriff Sparrow.

The image Earl drew of Amos Sparrow was straight out of a "Gunsmoke" episode or a Saturday matinee. The sheriff and his deputies all had ponytails and trimmed goatees and carried twin Colt cannons tied to their hips. Sparrow was said to answer to his own code of justice and had been censured numerous times by the state sheriff's association.

"What do you suggest?"

"Play your cards close to the vest."

"You're saying keep my distance?"

"If that means staying clear of Catawba County, the answer's yes."

"And if that doesn't work?"

"Do what every good citizen does. Call 911."

8

At their next session Patterson treated Falcon to lunch at the Elite Café, a Capital City favorite with legislators and the business crowd. The Casino Lounge was part of the café and known to aficionados as the venue for Hank Williams's last public performance while attending a musicians' union meeting there in December 1952.

They sat at a table near the back for privacy but were interrupted throughout the meal. Patterson knew everyone and they knew him. The café owner Mister "Pete" Xides stopped by the table to chat briefly and check on the service. Partway through lunch, as the crowd thinned, Falcon showed Patterson the flyer from the Convention Center parking lot and explained how he had come by it.

"Interesting," Patterson said but he couldn't see how it was connected to M's murder. He wasn't aware of any organization with that name. "It brings up Catawba County again. Now there's a connection that needs looking into." He didn't buy Earl Birdsong's warning to stay out of Catawba County—"If it's in Alabama we are obliged to go in it, through it, around it, or over it if need be! And that's a fact."

He handed the flyer back to Falcon and brought up his reason for the meeting. "Colonel, I feel we can write off our mystery man Sam Reuben. He's not only missing, he's an imposter, a complete fraud, or was. If the feds know what happened to him they aren't talking."

He explained that the men in dark suits who took custody

of Reuben's files when he disappeared were FBI agents. That could only mean one thing so he looked into the matter and learned that the Federal Marshal Service had relocated Reuben to Alabama under the witness protection program following the Mafia's Havana Conference of 1946. He was known to the mob as Joe "the Mouth" Romano. The Marshal Service gave him the pseudonym Sam Reuben as cover. He turned state's evidence against organized crime bosses and had looked over his shoulder all those years here in Alabama."

The information was hush-hush Patterson cautioned. It came from the local federal office responsible for keeping an eye on relocated witnesses in the event their cover was blown and were in eminent danger. If Reuben had a criminal record prior to relocating to Alabama that would explain why he gravitated to Phenix City where lawlessness had a free hand. The U.S. marshals presumably kept a watchful eye on him but claimed no knowledge that many of his clients had ties to organized crime or that his shady activities crossed the line into criminal culpability.

Such lax federal oversight was not new to Patterson. In the old days when Phenix City was known to high government officials as "the wickedest city in America" local FBI agents had looked the other way, even denying under oath the existence of illegal gambling or that criminal activity was unrestrained. They not only turned a blind eye to organized crime but took hands off when his father was murdered by corrupt state and local officials. Of course Reuben could have been a FBI plant and was playing both sides.

Reuben was not involved in the unwed mother case Patterson and his father had tried but he was reasonably certain of the man's wider ties to the adoption rackets—beyond his alleged part in M's victimization. He was suspected of having provided illegal brokering services which included forging documents and bribing public officials. The last documented mob threat to Reuben, the name

Joe Romano had appeared on a hit list found during the raid of the infamous Mafia summit in New York in 1957. Two decades had elapsed but there was no statute of limitations on squealers.

The mob finally exacted its revenge, the feds concluded, or Reuben skipped town one step ahead of a hired gun. The hitch in the latter theory was that he had not bothered to take a change of clothes and had made no bank withdrawals. As for the former if he was wearing cement shoes why hadn't anyone seen or heard anything and where was his baby pink Cadillac?

One thing that bothered the feds was Reuben's flamboyant lifestyle up until the time he disappeared. Despite a lack of steady income Reuben had a reputation for being a natty dresser and the pink Cadillac made him stand out like an Elvis impersonator. Maybe he figured he'd outlived the mobsters he ratted on or just didn't fear them anymore.

Patterson was not given access to the office files the FBI hauled away but his contacts assured him there was nothing in them pertaining to the once thriving baby mill in Phenix City. Reuben had covered his tracks too well. Patterson decided on another approach. There had been a coterie of attorneys in Phenix City who were on the mob's payroll before the crooked politicians were thrown out. These attorneys had represented the mob in all areas including the adoption rackets. Reuben would have worked with them and they would be privy to the cases he brokered.

Getting to this inside information was not cut and dried. All local attorneys who had done the mob's bidding, with one exception, had moved out of the state when the criminal empire crumpled in the aftermath of Albert Patterson's murder. The one former syndicate insider still practicing law in town was a colorful character named William G. Dollar. Pundits said the G stood for Greenback but most folks knew him as Bill Dollar—the latter often got turned around and he was called Dollar Bill. Even the circuit judge got it mixed up on occasion and referred to him as Counselor Greenback Dollar or Dollar Bill in court to everyone's amusement.

"The bottom line is we've found nothing yet to corroborate the story about Reuben's role in depriving M of her newborn child. Not that I don't believe her, I do. What happened to her fits precisely with our client's experience in the unwed mother case. We've got to go over to Phenix City and talk to Bill Dollar and squeeze the truth out of him."

They were so wrapped up in the Reuben story he almost forgot to ask Falcon what he'd turned up at the State Archives. Not much, Falcon allowed, except he had discovered convincing evidence that Luther and Tallulah Gooden who owned the huge estate in Catawba County were indeed Johnny Gooden's parents. They owned and published the weekly paper, the Catawba County Clarion, and Johnny Gooden's memorial service and burial was front-page news.

Falcon's revelation that Johnny Gooden had a son was not a surprise to Patterson. He too had been on the phone delving into the family history. "Yes, this does put a different perspective on things. I'm told when Luther and Tallulah died the grandson was heir to their fortune, every penny of it. It's said they now run a private hunting club on the estate, a club so exclusive nobody knows who the members are. They illegally brought in some exotic animals, and they're rumored to be doing a little mining up there for precious metals."

He nodded when Falcon suggested putting Catawba County on the itinerary despite Earl Birdsong's laconic advice. "Colonel, I agree with you but first things first. We have to get our ducks in a row before going near that estate without a warrant. We need to take a ride over to Phenix City and let me introduce you to a few folks including the loquacious Mister Dollar."

As they were leaving the Elite Café a black Cadillac sedan careened around the corner and barely missed them. There had been a downpour and they were splashed with rainwater. Stepping back to the curb Patterson's eyes widened as he stared after the speeding vehicle. "Do you believe in ghosts, Colonel?" he asked, regaining his balance. "Well, I've just seen one."

9

It was a lazy Saturday in downtown Phenix City. They were having a light breakfast with Major George Thunder at a small cafe up the street from where Patterson's father was slain. They had taken a back booth out of earshot but had patrons craning their necks. The former governor's presence sparked more than a little interest.

George Thunder had retrieved information from Army records that put an official stamp on the discovery Falcon made at the State Archives. The record of a son as Johnny Gooden's legal heir was as confusing to Thunder as it was to Falcon. Had M given birth to a son rather than a daughter—they had taken the child from her while she was under anesthesia and before she had a chance to see it—or could there be twins? Had even bigger lies been told? Thunder said the more he dug into the records the more red flags they raised.

The commander who signed the order shipping Johnny Gooden to Korea was Colonel Julius Summerfield, an Infantry officer now deceased. The widow Lucy Summerfield's annuity checks were sent to her at a nursing home in Hilton Head, South Carolina. That wasn't the end of it and Thunder wondered if the Colonel's role in the mystery was more than simply that of a martinet who sent an untrained soldier off to war to get a problem off his hands?

The records showed that Lucy Summerfield had given birth to a baby girl around the same time Johnny Gooden was killed in Korea. Thunder found it odd that this hadn't raised eyebrows at the time in view of Lucy Summerfield's advanced age and the fact that she had been barren in 30 years of marriage to the same husband. The birth certificate was on file in Georgia. Was it possible that Julius and Lucy Summerfield had adopted M's daughter and conspired to hide the fact? Or could the father have been a sperm donor? Falcon agreed it needed looking into.

Patterson had a question which at the moment seemed unrelated to their inquiry. He asked if Major Thunder remembered one-eyed Willie Abraham, the scourge of local surroundings in the Fifties. Thunder recognized the former sergeant's name and described him as the bad penny that never goes away. For Falcon's benefit they explained who they were talking about.

Willie Abraham was one of the highest decorated soldiers of the Korean War. He was stationed at Fort Benning before and after consecutive combat tours and had become a local celebrity of sorts. A loner who thrived on war and freaked out on peace Abraham boasted that he had more notches on his M-1 rifle than either Audie Murphy or Sergeant York. Then one night at Benning he got liquored up and cleaned out the NCO Club. He put the duty officer in the hospital when the military police tried to subdue him. He sat staring straight ahead showing no contrition at the court martial.

Life went downhill fast for Willie when he was booted out of the Army. A badly scarred face and glass eye resulted from vicious fist and knife fights around Columbus and Phenix City. The rampage ended one night in a roadside joint between Hattiesburg and Camp Shelby, Mississippi, when Willie got in a fight with a drunken weekend warrior and knifed him to death. His troubled past gave the prosecutors a slam-dunk at the trial. He was deemed to be incorrigible and the Judge handed down a life sentence without parole.

The last Patterson or Thunder heard about Abraham he was serving time in the Mississippi State Penitentiary at Parchman Farm and creating strife as the head of a white supremacist group when he reportedly was fatally shot by guards during a prison uprising.

Thunder's jaw dropped when Patterson said that Willie Abraham was not dead. "I saw him big as you please driving through downtown Montgomery. He nearly ran us down."

When they left the café Major Thunder had business back at Fort Benning while Patterson and Falcon planned to call on the last of the Sin City mouthpieces, the unctuous attorney Bill Dollar. They made a few stops along the way, nerve centers such as the county sheriff's office and city hall, where John Patterson knew everybody by their first names and introduced Falcon to so many people he would never remember their faces. From city hall they walked a couple of blocks over to Dollar's office.

The secretary announced their arrival over the intercom and out rushed a slightly rotund man wearing scuffed white and tan oxfords, light blue baggy seersucker suit, striped lavender shirt, and a rainbow of accoutrements—including red galluses that went out of style with Eugene Talmadge of Georgia. Patterson and Dollar had grown up in the same neighborhood but on different sides of the law. Patterson, like his father before him, had gone off to fight for his country in WWII while Dollar stayed back to corner a share of the black market shystering for the vice lords and the high rollers.

Dollar was effusive in welcoming the guests, his treble voice fluttering with excitement and rosy cheeks drowning in beads of sweat. "What a fine day for shucking corn, Governor." Dollar actually owned a farm but never shucked an ear of corn in his life, Patterson later told Falcon. There was a gold-plated replica of an ear of corn on Dollar's desk with a blue ribbon for winning first place at the county fair. Folks said he ordered the replica and blue ribbon from a seed company catalogue in Atlanta.

Patterson barely contained the contempt in his voice. He and his associate Colonel Falcon were working a couple of cold case files and believed that Dollar might be able to assist them. "Tell us what you know about the Gooden clan up in Catawba County and this

Sam Reuben fellow from Montgomery. We want the hard truth about that grandson of theirs and we're short on time and money."

Dollar fidgeted. He rubbed his jaw and squirmed in the over-stuffed faux leather chair. "Reuben, you say. You must be referring to that velvet-tongued Cadillac broker from Montgomery. He's somewhere out on the Yellow Brick Road I hear. And the Gooden family you said, that'd be Mister Luther and Missus Tallulah I surmise—they're the lord and lady of the manor up in Catawba County who perished in a fire a while back, but you know that. If I had their property I wouldn't be sitting here with you now, and that's a fact. You knew his granddaddy was a carpetbagger and snatched that land up for a pittance after the war."

Patterson's jaw tightened. "Don't beat around the bush with me, Bill Dollar. You and I've known each other since we wore knee pants. The Colonel and I drove all this way to see you and we've got business back in Montgomery."

"Maybe you could send a little of that business my way."

"Likely bring you more trouble than it's worth."

"Now, Governor, I could be putting my hunting license in jeopardy divulging privileged information without the other party's consent. You know that's so."

"I've got one of those hunting licenses too. Reckon we'll go on back to Montgomery and report on how cooperative you've been." Patterson rose up from the chair as if to leave.

Dollar jumped up to dissuade him. "No sir, Governor, I didn't say I wouldn't help you. I might have to purchase more health insurance when I do. Could you sweeten the pot just a little?"

"Not a thin dime. As Preacher R. K. Jones would say, bare your soul and get your reward in heaven."

Dollar was nervous, still fidgeting. He ran his pudgy hands through his thinning hair and rubbed the stubble on his chin. "You drive a hard bargain, Governor, I swear you do. Now if I repeat things that were told to me, not by clients you understand, that would not count as betraying a confidence, would it? I can't be held responsible for what other folks did?"

"I believe we understand each other. We'll just sit back in these fine chairs and bask in your hyperbole."

Falcon was a mere spectator in the exchange. He didn't understand the nuances of the conversation and was caught off guard when Dollar opened up and out poured a litany of transgressions. Dollar unloaded on Sam Reuben as a disgrace to the profession, a scalawag who scammed the very folks he was hired to represent. "The Gooden family retained that scoundrel in good faith. Their only son had been killed in Korea and they learned he may have fathered a child here in our fine city. They hired Reuben to find out the truth of the matter and if their son had fathered a child they wanted custody. Leastwise that's the way it was told to me."

Dollar was privy to a reliable informant that when Reuben came to Phenix City and found the mother-to-be was a young black woman he knew or thought he knew that she and the baby would be rejected by his clients and he would be out of a big commission. So he hit on an elaborate scheme to find another baby, a white one that was up for adoption and convince Luther and Tallulah Gooden that the white baby was their grandchild. To conceal the existence of their real grandchild of mixed race he acted to get the young black mother out of the picture and to sell her baby to other foster parents—thereby doubling his money with the two transactions.

He was assisted by lawyers aligned with the baby rackets and they convinced a pregnant white girl at a local brothel to go along with them. She was due to deliver her baby about the same time as Johnny Gooden's girlfriend which fit Reuben's plan perfectly. Before the Army brought the Gooden boy's body home from Korea and when the baby was about due, Reuben dressed the girl in her Sunday best and took her to meet the Gooden family at his office in Montgomery. The plan was to keep Luther and Tallulah away from Phenix City so they wouldn't stumble on the hoax.

From Dollar's account (he swore on his mother's grave he wasn't a party to the hoax) the Goodens were completely taken with the young woman who had them believing she was a Sunday school teacher and second-year student at Auburn University when she became pregnant with their son's child. Her parents were deeply religious, she claimed, and they refused to support her when they found out. She was desperate and had gone to the clinic to have an abortion but couldn't go through with it when she heard Johnny had been killed in the war. Reuben and a local lawyer had spurious documents drawn up to support her story.

Falcon didn't know what to believe but Patterson had heard it all before. The Kefauver Hearings had unveiled numerous stories so outrageous they strained credulity. "What happened to the young mother," he asked? Dollar scoffed. He said she was a pin cushion and kept pumping out babies like candy drops for the adoption hustlers until they were put out of business during the cleanup. There went her livelihood. One night she got in a bar fight, or so the story went, was badly cut up and left town. Dollar said folks doubted that story but were afraid to come right out and say it. She was one-eyed Willie Abraham's woman and it was whispered that he either beat her up or had it done.

"You see, Willie Abraham was the father of that baby she sold to the Gooden family. It was a blue-eyed boy the spitting image of Willie himself, when he had two good eyes." Willie was in Korea and when he came home he was fit to be tied because she had sold the baby and spent all the money including his share. After that whenever he got drunk, he'd beat her. He had finished his second combat tour when the war ended. Things didn't change when he got back and he eventually roughed her up so bad she feared for her life and moved to another state.

Patterson hadn't anticipated Willie Abraham's name coming up and now that it had he pursued the subject of Abraham's purported death. "Governor, you mean you don't know. Those Mississippi guards shot Willie, that's a fact, but they couldn't kill a legend like Willie. I hear he's out now, free as a bird. He's been spotted around the state driving a big Cadillac and smoking Cuban cigars."

On a brisk walk back to city hall where the car was parked Patterson took Falcon through the alley behind the Coulter Building where he once practiced law with this father. "Do you believe that fellow's story," Falcon asked.

"Every word, only he didn't implicate himself. I'd say he witnessed these events rather than being told about them. Bill Dollar's been waiting nigh on 30 years to tell that tale and he couldn't bring himself to admit his part in it."

When they reached the Coulter Building, Patterson pointed to a parking place behind the structure. "That's where they murdered my father. The cowards gunned him down and never gave him a chance. Crippled and mortally wounded he pulled himself out of the car and made it as far as the sidewalk over there where he fell in a pool of blood. He would approve of what you're doing, Colonel. He would help you set things straight."

They were both deep in thought on the drive back to Montgomery. They were much alike, this young former governor and his new fighter-pilot friend. Neither would step back from the precipice or think twice about righting old wrongs. Fight for all the right reasons or don't fight at all was a good rule of thumb. Patterson was first to break the silence. "We have a pattern developing, Colonel, and it's not a pretty one. Willie Abraham had such a frightful image, parents used his name to admonish their children when they got out of hand. That scalawag Bill Dollar seemed mighty nervous to me. He's afraid of something. I wonder what."

10

Falcon took off from Dannelly Field at daybreak and piloted the Cessna to Hilton Head, South Carolina. He had called the nursing home and the widow Lucy Summerfield agreed to see him. Arriving at the Hilton Head Airport he drove a rental car to the address on the outskirts of town. A nurse showed him to the visitor's lounge and an orderly wheeled in a mannish elderly woman who had been nervously awaiting his arrival.

At the receptionist's desk the nurse prepped Falcon that the widow Summerfield would be a difficult resident to interview, that she suffered chronic mental lapses and drifted in and out of reality. She had little or no contact outside the nursing home—Falcon was her only visitor in months—and she was presently in a confused state having spent a sleepless night going over in her mind what to say to him.

When they talked by phone she had been flustered and thought Falcon was calling with information about their daughter who had dropped out of college to protest the war in Vietnam and never came home. Now that he was there she gripped the arms of the wheelchair and asked what information he had about the daughter. Falcon's explanation that he had come there because he was searching for the daughter still failed to register and he had to prompt her more than once as they proceeded.

At one point she removed an album from a canvas pouch attached to the wheelchair and showed him pictures of the daughter, angelic when she was a child and a strikingly attractive young woman in college. "You can see she was special, not ours but we took her as our own. Julius and I couldn't have children so we adopted her when we were at Fort Benning, Georgia."

When Falcon raised the point that both her name and her late husband's name appeared falsely on the birth certificate as the natural parents and it was erroneously recorded in Georgia, she reacted with a blank stare. Julius handled such matters in their marriage and she left it all up to him, she said when pushed for a response. They obviously were not the natural parents but were listed as such on the birth certificate, according to what Julius told her, to keep the birth mother from having a change of heart and trying to get the baby back. She was to tell no one for fear it would cause her husband trouble with the Army.

More prodding from Falcon and she revealed that her husband felt responsible for the death of the baby's father when he was killed in Korea and the guilt was worse when Julius was in his cups. He started drinking heavily, she said, and was eager to adopt the baby when this man—she didn't know his name but the person she described was Sam Reuben—came to him with a story that the mother wanted to put her child up for adoption. "We were not allowed to meet with the mother because the man said it would be too hard on her. They were vultures. They took all of our money in the bank and we had to go in debt to pay what they charged us."

She and Julius named the daughter Peggy Sue after his grandmother. Peggy Sue was a precocious child and graduated from high school ahead of her age group. Her senior year she was the homecoming queen and valedictorian. "Julius was so proud of her and she capped her accomplishments by earning a full college scholarship." Apparently the daughter's freshman year went smoothly but that summer the Summerfield's observed a dramatic change in her attitude and the way she interacted with them.

One night when she was home from college, Julius had too much to drink and told Peggy Sue about her natural parents, the truth of her father's death in Korea and why her birth mother had given her up for adoption. A terrible row followed and the next day Peggy Sue left to go back to college. She told her parents she no longer wanted to be called Peggy Sue. She claimed to have hated her name since elementary school when Buddy Holly's rock and roll single of that name played on the jukeboxes.

The more alienated the daughter became the moodier and more disconsolate the spirit of Julius. He first blamed her alienation on the professors—they were teaching her what to think, not how to think—and finally he blamed himself the most. An Army psychiatrist suggested the daughter could be adopting a hippie persona because she was rebelling against his military lifestyle. Julius knew it was deeper than that. He began to drink more heavily than usual and one morning the wife couldn't awaken him. He had died in his sleep.

Julius was buried at Arlington National Cemetery. The daughter came to the funeral service with a college group in a psychedelic Volkswagen bus. A youthful looking professor was with them. That was the last time Lucy Summerfield saw the daughter. A high school classmate came by and told her that she had seen Peggy Sue at the Woodstock music festival in New York. She was with a group protesting the war in Vietnam. That was the summer of 1969. She returned to school but dropped out the following year. The widow Summerfield had heard nothing from her since.

It had taken most of the afternoon for Falcon to draw what little information he got from Lucy Summerfield but he was satisfied the results were worth the trip. She let him take a couple of the more recent pictures she had of the daughter and the names and addresses of acquaintances. Afterward he drove to the Oceanside and walked aimlessly along the beach, stopping at a kiosk to purchase a beer. Let the tide wash over his leather flight boots and the cuffs of his gabardine slacks. He had to shake off the drabness of that lonely room, breathe in the crisp salt air, and wash the bitter taste of acrimony from his lips.

The visit had given him an almost heady sensation that he was in reach of finding M's daughter, but who would he find when he did and would it lead to M's killer? He reflected on the daughter's rebellious spirit, as portrayed by Lucy Summerfield, and wondered if she had been among the shrill anti-war protesters that welcomed his generation home from Vietnam. He felt betrayed at the time. Now he wondered what had been missing in all those young lives, what injustices had they endured, and had their dreams of a more just world let them down? He was not ready to go there but what if history proved them right?

11

Upon returning to Montgomery Falcon took the pictures of Peggy Sue to the Department of Public Health to see if Susan, the employee who chased after him the last time he was there, recognized her. Susan thought hard before finally replying yes that looked like the young woman who came to the Department with one or more companions in a psychedelic Volkswagen bus. A few years had passed but she was certain it was the same person.

Satisfied that the pictures in his possession were of M's daughter he ran an ad in the Montgomery Advertiser offering a reward for information and had a printing shop run off flyers which he distributed around the Capital City. Shooter also carried flyers to Jasmine in Selma so she could pass them around her neighborhood. Falcon informed Earl Birdsong what they were doing and that Jasmine was helping out.

Earl wasn't convinced. Grumpy old Earl: "My boys think you're being manipulated. Who else had motive, opportunity. She could be helping find the daughter so she can do her in too."

"I'm still here, aren't I?" Falcon hung up on Earl and used the phone to try and run down the daughter's former college friends. With the names and addresses that Lucy Summerfield gave him, he succeeded in getting some additional information about the daughter but not a clue to her present whereabouts. Collectively her friends painted a portrait of a bright, talented young woman who cloaked her beauty in Gypsy clothes and had an almost desperate need to fill a void in her life and discover who she really was. Each voiced the opinion that alone or perhaps with others of her group she had gone on the road to try and find her natural parents.

The plot thickened with these snippets of information. Falcon now had convincing evidence that M's daughter had come to Montgomery seeking information about her birth parents. This was before M returned from Europe so their paths had not crossed. But the odds were even that she could have made contact with her paternal grandparents, Luther and Tallulah Gooden.

According to Lucy Summerfield, her husband divulged to their daughter who her natural parents were and the circumstances of her father's death. But Colonel Summerfield had no information about the birth mother and no earthly idea where she was. Furthermore, neither of the natural parents appeared on the birth certificate which was filed in Georgia. What then had persuaded M's daughter's to put Montgomery on her road map?

Had she gone to Columbus, Georgia, and Phenix City first? That made sense although no one, not even Bill Dollar, had mentioned seeing her. But then why would he? If all she had to go on were the clues divulged by her foster parents, they would be enough to eventually track down her paternal grandparents. But would they accept her? She had no proof, only her foster father's word. If she had indeed come south and failed in the search for her birth mother and the grandparents refused to recognize her as their legitimate grandchild, she could be anywhere on the globe by now.

He was sitting at the bar thinking that another trip to Phenix City might be in the offing when a call came in from Patterson's secretary. Her boss was in court today defending a client and instructed her to call Falcon and give him the news that Attorney Bill Dollar over in Phenix City had gone missing. That's all she knew except her boss thought Falcon might want to drive over there and use Patterson's name to inquire around city hall and the sheriff's office to see if Dollar's disappearance had anything to do with their visit and the inquiry into M's murder.

That evening he received a call back from a woman who was Peggy Sue's roommate at the university. Her married name was Betty Lou Dowd but because of her sunny disposition and golden locks everybody called her Tangerine. She wasn't much help. It had been years since she heard from her former roommate. Peggy Sue was with her boyfriend, an assistant professor at the University, and they were touring the country in a beat-up hippie bus. They sent a postcard from Gulf Shores, Alabama. All it said was "Wish you were here."

12

Before leaving the next morning Falcon phoned Earl Birdsong to tell him he was working on a new angle in M's murder and would be going to Phenix City to see if it had legs. He figured it was none of Earl's affair but he wanted to get back on the Chief Detective's good side. Earl knew already. "Does it have anything to do with that fellow Dollar's disappearance?"

Patterson had phoned Sheriff Breedlove in Russell County and other local officials and they were expecting Falcon's visit. Apparently the sheriff had let Earl in on the news. Falcon brought some of the flyers with him and Breedlove said he would be glad to show them around.

They drove out to Bill Dollar's house to talk with the wife. She was hysterical most of the night and the doctor had prescribed sedatives to calm her down. All she knew was her husband took their poodle for a walk a little before midnight. The poodle came home. The husband didn't.

The sheriff and his deputies had scoured the neighborhood. There were no signs of a struggle anywhere. A couple up the street heard tires screeching and a vehicle taking off in the middle of the night but didn't recall what time it was. None of the other neighbors heard a thing.

They went by Dollar's office. The secretary was there. She jumped every time the phone rang thinking it might be her boss or a kidnapper demanding ransom. She said he had acted jittery the day he disappeared but that was all. On a whim Falcon showed her one of the flyers he brought with him and asked if she had ever seen the woman in the picture. To jog her memory he said the woman would have been with a man and maybe others in a psychedelic Volkswagen bus.

The secretary was new to the job and hadn't seen the woman before. The sheriff asked to see the flyer again. He hadn't recognized the woman when Falcon handed him the flyers back at the office but the mention of a psychedelic bus triggered his memory. "It's been a few years but the hippies driving that crazy bus created quite a stir when they came to town. I read in the Columbus Ledger where they ran them off the reservation over at Fort Benning." He took a closer look at the flyer and thought that could be the woman in the bus, only she was dressed differently. "Like a gypsy," he said.

He also remembered the couple causing a scene at the local hospital. One of his deputies responded to the hospital's 911 call and the couple had already gone when he got there. "It had something to do with the woman's birth certificate. She had been told that she was born in the hospital and they had no record of it. Something along that line, as I recall."

They spent the day talking to a variety of people including nurses at the hospital without coming up with additional information about the woman in the picture or Bill Dollar's disappearance. The sheriff said to give his best regards to the former governor and promised he would let them know if anything new came up concerning either person of interest. He hinted that their next move might be to drag the bottom of the Chattahoochee.

The sun had gone down and the top was up on the convertible. It had been sitting all day in the parking lot behind city hall and a pop-up shower that cooled things off was welcome. The seats were still warm and the engine started right up. He turned the radio dial to a country music station and headed out to the highway. Johnny Cash was singing "Don't Take Your Guns to Town." Falcon was thrumming his fingers on the steering wheel and singing along with Cash and the Tennessee Three. A drizzling mist fogged the windshield and the wipers were on

All said, it had been a good day. At least he knew that M's daughter had been in the area. He wondered if they would find Bill Dollar and Sam Reuben together on a tropical island somewhere, or were they swimming with the fish in the Chattahoochee. He took his eyes off the road for an instant, as Cash and the Tennessee Three hit a high note, when it happened. Another vehicle swerved in front of the convertible, cutting him off. He hit the brakes. They were squishy and then nothing. He woke up in the Tuskegee Hospital with a broken nose, bruised ribs and a mild concussion. The convertible was on its side in a farmer's haystack

13

The hospital released him the next day but the convertible required major repairs. If not for the farmer's demolished haystack, which the insurance company refused to cover, the convertible would have been totaled. The garage gave him the use of a loaner, a 12-year-old banged-up Ford Mustang, but he had to put down a deposit and pay for the gas that was in the tank. Someone had tampered with the brakes on the convertible while parked in plain view behind city hall—leaving him a souvenir of the old Sin City.

He preferred to keep what happened under wraps but the broken nose and the previously wrecked first generation Mustang gave him away. He briefed Patterson and Earl over the phone and brushed it aside when anyone else asked what happened. "Just wanted to get in the saddle and ride one of those wild ponies again, that's all there is to tell."

A mysterious call came in while he was trading barbs with Shooter at the bar. No pretense was made to disguise the stranger's voice on the other end of the line.

"Mr. Falcon?"

"Speaking."

"Mr. Jake Falcon?"

"Guilty."

"I have a message for you, Mr. Falcon. Listen carefully. What I have to say concerns your health."

The caller proceeded with instructions for Falcon to meet a private plane at an abandoned landing strip south of Montgomery at midnight. The plane would be on the ground no longer than 30 minutes to refuel. The caller issued precise directions. Falcon would drive down I-65 to a designated turnoff onto a backcountry road leading to the landing strip. He would come alone. A security guard would be expecting him and would take him aboard the plane to meet with an unnamed VIP. "Be there," the caller said and hung up the phone.

The threat was implicit. Falcon's initial reaction was for the caller to blow it out his ear, but curiosity got the better of him. It could be a hoax; it could be the FBI or the CIA; it could be most anything. He tried to reach Patterson at his office but he had left early to teach a class at Troy University. Falcon left a cryptic message with the secretary concerning the meeting at the abandoned air strip and said he would brief her boss when they got back together.

It was pitch-black as he made his way down the twisting, thinly graveled back road to the airstrip—with the Mustang bouncing and chugging along as if it had been broken in on dirt roads with dangerous curves and deep ruts. As he approached the weed-grown strip he could see they were using smudge pots and high beams to light the way for planes landing there—a smuggler's hideaway flaunting FAA regulations and most likely guilty of wrongdoing far more sinister. Following instructions he dimmed the headlights as he approached a cemented area serving as a tarmac and the security guard signaled with a flashlight where to park.

The plane was on the ground and preparing to refuel. An Army surplus tanker truck had pulled up beside it. The guard patted Falcon down and confiscated the Beretta and a small tape recorder Falcon always carried with him. "These will be returned when you exit the plane." The guard stepped back and Falcon went aboard.

"Welcome, Mr. Falcon. I'm pleased you came." The nondescript elderly figure seated across the table in the dim lighting midway down the aisle motioned for his guest to take a seat. The man was dressed in a loose fitting suit and tennis shoes—comfort had trumped style. His thinning white hair and collar were rumpled from having napped. On the street he could pass as the kindly grandfather figure next door, the senior citizen at the corner thrift shop or the owner of the candy store down the street. Then he took off the dark glasses. His eyes were as lifeless as a stick of gum.

The man looked vaguely familiar. Perhaps he appeared on the evening news or a wanted poster. Falcon was politely curious. "I didn't catch your name, mister …." The man smiled. "I didn't give it." He edged a paper bag across the table while commending Falcon for being a concerned citizen and helping to locate members of the extended family. The family understands you lost your client and took this case without a retainer. He responded to the surprised look on Falcon's face: "Yes, we do have a long reach."

He said the family was feeling the heat from the FBI over the disappearance of Joe "the Mouth" Romano, a.k.a. Sam Reuben, and now the pressure would be twice the nuisance with the Phenix City mouthpiece missing. The family wanted to show its appreciation for Falcon's efforts in finding out what happened to the two men. All he had to do in return was to notify the family first when the two men turned up, either dead or alive. Falcon pushed the bag back across the table. He did not mean to be discourteous or unappreciative, he said, but he could not accept payment for something he was not at liberty to do.

Falcon's only interest in the two missing men was their connection to his murdered client and the whereabouts of her daughter. If he solved these two mysteries without knowing what happened to Reuben and Dollar that would be the end of it. Besides, he was in lock step with the local authorities on the case and they were in sync with his every move.

The man smiled again. Over the table or under the table, he said, it was hard to deal with a person of principle. He was not sure if standing on principle was a strength or weakness but the family respected that in a man. He gave his assurances that the family had nothing to do with the disappearance of Reuben or Dollar or with the dead bodies turning up. "The turf wars went out with the speakeasies. Those special privileges are reserved for bigger fish like Bugsy Siegel. You're dealing with punks." They were no competition to the family, but he admitted that sometimes gnats had to be swatted too.

He thanked Falcon for coming to see him and held up two hands to signal their talk was over. "The reward will be kept in escrow should you change your mind. It could go to your favorite charity, you know."

Falcon departed the plane under the watchful eye of the security guard, who returned the Beretta and tape recorder. He was still sorting it all out in his mind as he headed back to town the way he came. Large drops of rain spattered the windshield. Thunderclouds were building. Looking over his shoulder he watched the plane lift off and circle the now dark field, and then the skies swallowed the plane up ahead of a long black veil of thunder and lightning. He drove as fast as he safely could to get off the narrow, winding road before the heavy rains came.

<h1 style="text-align:center">14</h1>

When he debriefed Earl Birdsong on the landing strip rendezvous Earl figured the secluded field had to be a drop off for contraband. The so-called family apparently flew into the field on a regular basis and took advantage of its locality to size Falcon up and see where he stood and how much he knew. They obviously had Falcon on their radar screen and were aware of his movements.

Earl notified the local FBI office but they expressed no interest. They doubted his suspicions the field was used on a regular basis. The syndicate was smarter than that. They had hundreds of landing strips available to them across the country. Rarely did they land at one twice in the same month or over a longer period if the field's use had been compromised. The feds didn't have the manpower for surveillance of all the landing strips, and to single one out with no intelligence a drop was planned would be folly.

Patterson agreed the landing strip was likely used for smuggling drugs or other contraband. It sounded as if smugglers had found themselves in some perceived turf war and were trying to figure out how Falcon fit into the puzzle. They could've been fishing for more information or trying to get Falcon to back off. "They may have been testing you," Patterson said. "If you had taken that money they would either have their hooks in you or you would never see them again."

Of more immediate concern was Falcon's accident as he was leaving Phenix City. Patterson was certain that outsiders were responsible for sabotaging the brakes on the convertible and it had to be a professional job to have escaped notice. It didn't seem likely that the family was responsible since they contacted Falcon so soon after the fact. Patterson thought it might be tied to Falcon's search for M's daughter or he had stumbled onto something bigger.

Patterson and his wife Tina had dropped by the hotel bar the night before and barely missed Falcon who left to keep the midnight rendezvous. They were on the way home from teaching his night class at Troy University and didn't stay long upon learning that Falcon was not at the bar. Shooter was on cloud nine. All eyes were on the popular couple, he said, and it sucked the oxygen out of the room when they left.

Meanwhile calls had come in from people who saw the flyer bearing M's daughter's picture, but nothing of substance. Jasmine's flyer campaign had spread across a wide area beyond Dallas County and the night after Falcon went to the landing strip her family became distraught and contacted Shooter when she failed to return home. Falcon leaned on Earl Birdsong and he put out an APB to try and find her.

Falcon and Shooter blamed themselves for getting Jasmine involved. Both were nursing mild hangovers when morning came and Birdsong called to tell them she'd been found. "What was she doing in Catawba County? They have her behind bars charged with loitering and littering."

Birdsong said he had talked with Sheriff Sparrow and Falcon could secure Jasmine's release by going to Catawba County and paying her fine. He didn't know how much the fine was but felt certain from his limited experience with county officials there it would be steep. They had no standard fees and the Justice of the Peace, Judge Mose Henry, levied fines according to what he figured folks could pay.

"He's a tough old bird and he'll leave a hole in your pocket. Go alone and take your checkbook. Don't go up there and be caustic or unfriendly whatever you do." He didn't want to get another call to come up and bail Falcon out too.

Falcon burned the road up in the old loaner he was driving until he crossed the Catawba County line and slowed to a crawl. Speed limits weren't posted and he wasn't going to take a chance on exceeding them. Of course that wasn't a sure thing in a JP court for they were known to fine offenders, and especially strangers, for going too slow on the open road—all according to the judge's state of mind and where the speed traps were.

A camouflaged truck with oversized tires pulled out from behind a clump of trees and followed him into town. When he parked in front of the sheriff's office the truck continued down Main Street to a small country store. Falcon spotted a similar truck parked behind the sheriff's office. He figured an uncle or a cousin owned the dealership.

Sheriff Sparrow impressed Falcon as the most slovenly appearing lawman he'd ever laid eyes on. He was 5 feet 10 inches tall, boney, and beady eyed. His face was pimply with dimpled chin, goatee, and greasy hair pulled back into a ponytail held in place by a rubber band. His uniform was wrinkled and dirty. His six-guns were hanging on the wall behind him. He didn't look up when Falcon entered.

"Are you Sheriff Amos Sparrow?"

"Who's asking?"

"The name's Jake Falcon."

"I know who you are. You come for your girl?" The sheriff explained that his deputies had him in their sights the minute he crossed the county line.

"Earl Birdsong called you?"

"He said nothing about you being a white boy."

"That a problem, Sheriff?"

"Not unless you make it one?"

Falcon heeded Birdsong's advice and kept his cool. Sparrow had a deputy bring Jasmine from her cell and they piled in a squad car and drove out to Judge Henry's place. They traveled several miles east of town away from the Mississippi line, heading down a winding gravel road parallel to the main highway covered on both sides by thick woods fenced in by barbed wire with no-trespassing signs strung out as far as the eye could see. The signs brought to mind a verse in Woody Guthrie's "This Land is Your Land" and had Falcon humming the tune until growing silent under a harsh glare from Amos Sparrow.

Judge Mose Henry knew they were coming but kept them waiting for the pleasure it gave him and to show his authority. The judge had a history of eccentricity on the bench and had been censured or suspended on more than one occasion for quirky behavior bordering on misconduct. He was taller than the sheriff and ganglier. His place was a small patch of land overrun by weeds and piglets and clucking Rhode Island Reds—altogether a scene of rustic tranquility and benign neglect.

Off to the side were freshly plowed rows and a stand of corn watched over by a fully dressed scarecrow and Judge Henry hidden from view and brandishing a double-barreled shotgun. They walked up to the porch of the weathered frame house and he startled them when he fired both barrels into the air from the direction of the corn rows and emerged carrying a string of dead crows slung over his shoulder and cussing because his last shots had missed. He was dressed in overalls, a denim shirt, and brogans, and needed a shave. The tranquility had been an illusion. The neglect was real.

Three Doberman pinschers guarded the judge, one on each side and one to the rear as he approached the front porch. The Dobermans followed onto the porch and took their positions around him as he pulled up a rocker and plopped down.

"You boys like blackbird soufflé?" he asked.

"Thanks all the same but we already ate, your honor." Sparrow answered for the group.

"You won't change your mind? Eat a little crow is good for the constitution, teaches respect and humility." He looked Falcon over with a toothless grin. "Isn't that right, boy?"

When Falcon didn't respond, Judge Henry's jaw tightened. "Are you hard of hearing, boy?"

"Sorry, your honor, were you addressing me?"

"You bet your sweet ass I was." Judge Henry bristled.

Sparrow, to his credit, saw where the conversation was going and tried to head it off. "Your honor, this young woman broke the law. Colonel Falcon is here to pay the fine."

When Judge Henry's demeanor didn't change, Sparrow tried again. "What are you planning on doing with them crows, your honor?"

"Thought we'd feed them to your inmates down at the jail."

"We got no inmates but this young woman."

"Well?"

"And she goes free when her fine is paid."

"Then I'll feed them to my blue ribbon sows."

"That's a capital idea, your honor."

"They'll be eating high on the hog so to speak."

Judge Henry had the last word and stomped into the house to change into more formal attire, leaving the Doberman triumvirate to guard the porch. When he came back out he was still wearing the overalls and denim shirt but had donned a tattered long black coat with tails and a dark bowtie. He belatedly acknowledged Jasmine's presence with a lecherous grin and turned to Falcon.

"Big city detective, I hear they found one of you boys at the bottom of the Chattahoochee."

"So I hear."

"You're not looking for that kind of trouble, are you?"

"I certainly hope not."

"Your honor, you forgot to say your honor."

Judge Henry's face was a full moon as he turned his attention on Falcon and lectured him. "I can tell you got spunk, boy. I like that in a man. Trouble is, spunk can get a stranger in serious trouble in these parts. You got to follow the yellow line and don't stray off onto the shoulders. Keep your bladder under control at all times. You so much as piss on a rock, that's breaking the law and will get you a healthy fine. You get my drift, boy?"

Before Falcon could speak up, they were distracted by movement at the corner of the house and a small child stepped into the open and stared at them with large, inquisitive eyes. Jasmine and Falcon stared back in awe. She was an enchanting child with a natural tan and long pigtails, possibly of mixed blood it was hard to tell, and wearing a print dress. She was totally out of place, an uncut diamond in a setting of squalor.

Judge Henry shushed her away. "Get on inside, girl, or go out back and play." She slipped away obediently, sidling along the wall to the back of the house.

Judge Henry, having left his shotgun and gavel inside, pulled a heavy revolver out of its holster slung over the back of the rocking chair and pounded the butt on the porch to call the proceedings to order. The judge knew his firearms. Falcon recognized the revolver as a replica of the Colt 1851 Navy Revolver, a favored weapon of the Confederacy. Sheriff Sparrow had heard it all before and he stared off into space when Judge Henry took a deep breath and continued to lecture his captive audience.

"On your way out here you saw there wasn't a solitary structure between here and town. That's because the sun rises and sets on Gooden land in all directions from one end of the county to the other. Those no trespassing signs mean what they say. You want to resist the temptation to pull over to the side of the road and go into the woods to relieve yourself or to look around. A person can get lost back in those woods and never be found. They have a big hunting lodge and you'll likely be mistaken as their next prey."

Judge Henry placed one hand on the Bible and the other over his heart. "I swear this court is colorblind, fair to a fault, and stubborn as a mule. To intruders we might seem a might peculiar. Everybody knows they don't teach eccentricity in law school. It's in our DNA. Show me twelve different judges and I'll show you a dozen different opinions. And you don't even have a say in picking your trial judge. What's not eccentric in that?

"Mind you the courtroom has always been good theater. Judges chastise you, sentence you, some even preach to you. If folks want a sermon they can go to church on Sunday. Judge Roy Bean would love TV cameras in the courtroom. One day you'll be reading books about me and watching movies about me like they do Judge Roy Bean. Wouldn't surprise me none if they have college professors over at the University working on that right now. They say Judge Roy Bean banged the daughters and hanged the sons. Don't tell me it's not good theater."

Without warning Judge Henry swung the pistol around and fired into the yard dropping a Rhode Island Red in its tracks and sending the other clucking hens and squealing piglets scurrying for cover. He pointed to the fallen Red and one of the guard dogs fetched the dead hen and dropped it at the master's feet. Judge Henry laid the pistol down. "It causes a bit of commotion but this way Miss Lillie won't have to pick the buckshot out. She loves fried chicken but my store-bought teeth can't take that buckshot."

Falcon hadn't flinched when the bullet sung past his shoulder, although he later admitted to Shooter that he damn near fainted and then became visibly shaken when Judge Henry pounded the porch and assessed the fine—"seven hundred big ones cash or check and the defendant goes with you to Montgomery. Otherwise we'll get her a mop and bucket and she can clean up that outhouse the sheriff calls a jail."

Judge Henry adjourned the court and went in the house without another word. The Dobermans followed them out to the cars and sat watching them leave. The scene was surreal. Nothing he had just witnessed was what it seemed. The guard dogs were professionally trained and the judge was not the hick he purported to be. Was he putting on an act? If so, why and did this have anything to do with M's daughter? Was Judge Henry the center of gravity? He would have you think that, but Falcon wasn't buying it. They were all dancing to someone else's music.

15

Sheriff Sparrow waited until Falcon had paid the fine and then told him there were more charges. Jasmine's car had been impounded and his deputies couldn't get it started. She could leave it and it would be abandoned and put on the auction block, or the sheriff could have it repaired and towed back to Montgomery. The charges would be fifty dollars to get it released and three times that for repairs and towing. "Just make the check out to Sparrow's Garage. My nephew will do you right."

"Are brakes his specialty?" Falcon asked. Sparrow shot him a nasty look but before the sheriff could say anything a deputy came in and whispered in his ear. The sheriff dropped both checks in his desk drawer, strapped on his guns and took a rifle off the wall. "Put out an APD and call out the hounds! We got a runner on the loose!" He brushed past Falcon and Jasmine and rushed out the door.

A deputy escorted the Mustang to the county line in a camouflaged pickup. The front tag bore the iconic Confederate soldier vowing to "Forget, Hell." The truck turned back when they crossed into the next county and Falcon pulled into a McDonald's down the highway. Jasmine hadn't eaten since the night before and was starved.

She had spoken no more than a couple of sentences since Falcon arrived to bail her out, and she was still reticent inside McDonald's. Other customers ignored them for the most part but there were a few whispered asides and smug faces. When she was back in the car Jasmine opened up with a few choice words of her own. She had not been physically abused behind bars but she was subjected to verbal harassment and humiliation.

The sheriff had refused to let her make a telephone call and Jasmine believed they would have kept her locked up or worse had Earl Birdsong not put out the APB on her. Before that she had made up a story that she was working with the Montgomery police when she posted the flyers. Sparrow said that cut no ice with him, this was his jurisdiction and they could go suck on a lemon. He thought better of it when he heard the APB on the police channel and called to let Birdsong know she was there.

Jasmine was concerned about the fate of a teenage Mexican girl who shared the cell with her and wondered if there was anything they could do to help. "I'm afraid something bad may have happened to her." The girl spoke enough broken English for Jasmine to understand her and she claimed to have been raped by her jailers.

The girl's name was Cristina. She worked in the mess hall and was in jail for stealing food for her family. She told a story of having been smuggled across the border with her family and other Mexican laborers. She was a young girl at the time and remembered being herded into the back of a van and driven across country to Alabama where their captors forced them to work on this big farm. Her parents called the smugglers Coyotes. The laborers lived in squalor on the farm and she described working conditions that were akin to slave labor.

"Did she mention the Gooden estate?"

"She didn't know the farm's name."

"What kind of farming?"

"They were growing pot, marijuana."

"That's all?"

"Acres of it, she said, and there were meth labs." The girl had described to Jasmine a large-scale drug smuggling operation as well. She claimed there was a small landing strip on the farm and the smugglers brought in loads of cocaine by truck and by plane. She said the laborers were terrified of the smugglers and believed they were part of the Mexican cartels.

The girl heard rumors of a hunting club and a military-style training area hidden by the woods in the backside of the farm. The sounds of gunfire and explosions coming from behind the woods were a daily reminder of the dangers the laborers faced. "She said people have been killed there."

"Her story seems far-fetched."

"That's what I told her."

"And her reply was?"

"There are many graves."

16

They drove the rest of the way in silence. Falcon dropped Jasmine off at her relative's house in Selma and stopped long enough to phone Birdsong and Shooter to let them know she was safe at home. Jasmine remembered one other item she thought Falcon should know. The jailers confiscated the flyers she had with her but they overlooked one that was folded in her pocket. The Mexican girl said she had not seen the woman in the picture but kept the flyer so she could show it around when she got out of jail.

Falcon was reluctant to repeat the jailed girl's allegations without proof. He felt he had to bring Earl Birdsong in on the allegations but wanted to discuss strategy with Patterson first. Patterson was busy with a client and Falcon cooled his heels until they finished. When Falcon briefed him on the day's activities Patterson didn't seem surprised. "We may have stirred up a hornet's nest if only part of what she says is true."

Patterson wanted to think things through and feel out a couple of trusted associates on the veracity of the accusations made by the girl. This matter was too serious to sit on and too dangerous to widen the circle of inclusion if it meant putting the girl's life in jeopardy. He would leave the decision to inform Chief Detective Birdsong to Falcon, but cautioned that public offices are obliged to inform their superiors and in a bureaucratic chain of command little is left to privacy.

Judge Henry's rambling discourse on eccentricity and the judiciary brought to mind the old Phenix City days when the going price for the bench was the same as that for the witness stand and the jury box. Patterson thought egocentricity might be a more proper reference than eccentricity. "Don't sell Mose Henry short though. He used to play the mandolin and has been on and off the bench so many times they call him the minstrel judge. He's flexible if nothing else and may be the only tame beast in that menagerie."

Birdsong's heart was willing but his hands were tied. Falcon had decided to share the allegations with Earl without revealing his source. The alleged drug operations, human trafficking, virtual enslavement of Mexican laborers, and murder were matters of urgency and too hot for Falcon to handle alone. He feared for the Mexican girl's life. Barbarians who committed such crimes were capable of anything. Birdsong knew what the answer would be but agreed to contact the Justice Department anyway.

He wasn't surprised when the Justice Department spokesman laughed in his face. For them to conduct a raid on such wild, unsubstantiated claims by a third party was out of the question. No federal judge in the land would issue a warrant under these circumstances. The Department would take the matter under advisement and open an investigation only if there was hard evidence of federal crimes being committed. To Birdsong and Falcon that meant nothing would be done.

Falcon had no choice but to act. Was there anyone in Catawba County he could trust? The people in and around the county would have to be blind not to know what was going on there. He couldn't take on the whole county so the only option open to him was to obtain the proof required to move the feds out of their easy chairs. Birdsong didn't like the glint in his eye. "You have to leave this to the proper authorities," he cautioned.

That evening John and Tina Patterson came by the hotel bar to let Falcon know they would be gone for several days. They were leaving the next day to fly to New York City on business. Their plans were to stay at the Waldorf Astoria and journey on to Europe to visit Tina's family before returning home. Patterson gave him the addresses and telephone numbers where they could be reached in an emergency.

Falcon's restless energy and the available courses of action were easy signs to read. Beneath that tough fighter pilot exterior beat the heart of a nonconformist. He had never been at ease issuing orders or was overly keen on following them. A flight leader had noted this on his efficiency report in Vietnam, but the wing commander marked through it and wrote that Falcon's instinctive roll of the dice was an effective "I lead, you follow" tactic—it gave the enemy fits and hadn't got him or his wing man killed yet.

The efficiency report stressed that Falcon carried out the assigned missions with the best of them, pressed hard and was always on target. Could be that Patterson, like the wing commander, knew him better than Falcon knew himself. Patterson sensed that Falcon wouldn't sit on his hands while they were gone. All he said was, "When you see Judge Henry ask if he remembers me?"

17

Could he go back to Catawba County so soon without raising suspicion? Probably not, but oh well, life's a gamble. Those thoughts toyed with the correctness of his decision as he ordered a breakfast sandwich and coffee at the McDonald's he and Jasmine had stopped at before. Not that his body craved nourishment but his arms and shoulders needed a break from the power steering going out on the loaner.

Looking out the window he caught a glimpse of a thin, dark-skinned lad who looked to be a teenager digging through the Dumpster. Later as he drove off and looked back he saw the boy scurrying into a bushy area behind McDonald's. The boy clutched the bag of sausage burritos and hash browns that Falcon placed next to the Dumpster before driving away. He hoped the few bills he left at the bottom of the bag did not go unnoticed.

Up the road after crossing the county line he pulled into a gas station and paid the attendant to add power steering fluid. One of the sheriff's deputies pulled alongside in a camouflaged pickup and asked where he was headed. When he said he was on the way to Sheriff Sparrow's office, the deputy said to follow him.

The sheriff and his deputies were in a dither over a police alert and they were not pleased to see Falcon. When asked why he was there Falcon replied that he was interested in joining the exclusive hunting club he was told about when bailing Jasmine out of jail. Sparrow's muffled response dripped with sarcasm. "What don't you city boys understand about exclusive? Where I come from sport that means you have to be invited."

Sparrow said recruiting was Judge Henry's bailiwick and ordered one of his deputies to lead Falcon out to the judge's house. Unlike last time the judge was not expecting them. Sparrow was distracted and forgot to call ahead. Judge Henry was on the porch in his rocking chair sipping on Jack Daniels Old No. 7. The Doberman's were out on the back forty taking their morning run. The piglets were penned up in back and he was tossing kernels of corn to the Rhode Island Reds. "Howdy boys, are you delivering my morning paper? Or is it a fool's errand?"

A wry grin from Falcon—you couldn't ignore the theater in the man. The deputy excused himself, saying he had to get back, but Judge Henry said no, you boys sit and talk a spell. He called out the name Cristina and a young Latino woman came to the door. He instructed her to bring a pitcher of iced tea for his guests. "I would offer you boys some of this fine Tennessee sour mash but you're both driving."

The noise attracted the mysterious child Falcon had seen the last time. She was staring at them from the corner of the house again with those large inquisitive eyes. Unnoticed by Judge Henry she scooted under the porch where she could observe them and hear every word. The presence of the child from last time had haunted him but he neglected to bring the subject up with either Patterson or Jasmine. She obviously was not the judge's child. What was she doing there?

Cristina brought the iced tea and afterward Falcon saw her standing inside by the screen door staring his way. Jasmine had mentioned that her teenage cellmate's name was Cristina and he wondered if this was she. That was resolved in his mind when Judge Henry remarked to the deputy how much he and Miss Lillie appreciated them releasing the girl into his custody and they just might keep the little lady. "Tell the sheriff he outdid himself this time and we're a might grateful. We truly are. "

The rustle of Cristina's skirt at the door caught the judge's attention. "Get back inside, girl. Go look in on Miss Lillie. She's awake and might crave a little cha-cha-cha before breakfast." The girl gave him a puzzled look and disappeared inside.

"Now what's your business Mr. Falcon? What brought you all the way back up here to see us?"

"I like to hunt."

"That's not against the scripture, long as it's not on Sunday."

"And I'm not shooting somebody."

"I was just going to say."

"I've heard good things about your hunting club."

"You don't say."

"And I would like to become a member."

"Well, you can't. So you drove all the way up here for nothing."

Judge Henry explained that there was a waiting list as long as Falcon's arm and there wouldn't be any openings anytime soon. Plus he would have to undergo a thorough investigation and that would take more time. "I would just go on back to where you came from and give up thinking about the hunting club if I was you." He stood up to go inside. "Now if that's all."

"Before I forget, an acquaintance sends his regards."

"Who's that?"

"John Patterson."

"Did he now?"

"He wasn't sure you'd remember him."

"He didn't get my vote, if that's what you mean."

The judge said he had to go look in on Miss Lillie. She'd been feeling poorly of late. "You boys can show yourself out." When he went inside the small girl came out from under the porch and ran to the back of the house. They were left sitting on the porch steps drinking iced tea.

Leaving the premises they split at the crossroads, the deputy heading back to the sheriff's office and Falcon taking the turn-off to Montgomery. When he came to the familiar McDonald's he parked near the Dumpster, cracked the windows and left the car doors unlocked. He ordered two milk shakes and kept an eye on the Mustang while the woman behind the counter filled the order.

Back on the road he drove until he felt they were far enough away from Catawba County to feel safe and pulled over to the shoulder. He held one of the milk shakes over the front seat to the rear and said, "You can come out now." When there was no movement he repeated the sentence in broken English and the thin, dark-skinned lad crawled out from under a serape on the back floorboard and took the milk shake.

Falcon had observed the boy slipping from the bushes and getting into the back seat. He assumed early on that the boy was Sheriff Sparrow's missing prisoner and wanted to help him avoid capture. The sheriff's frantic response to the boy's escape gave the impression that a dangerous fugitive was on the loose. The appearance of the frightened teenager cowering in the back seat of the Mustang disputed that. The situation convinced Falcon that the only threat the boy posed had nothing to do with breaking the law and everything to do with what he knew.

18

The boy's name was Juan. His sister was Cristina, the young woman who had been jailed for stealing food and was now at Judge Henry's place. He had no money and no plan but had run away from the estate with the hope of finding help for his sister. His pleas to overseers at the estate had been met with snorts of contempt. They left him with no choice but to seek outside help.

Falcon was eager to hear Juan's story but first he had to be fed and given a place of refuge. The Piedmont bar was open and Shooter ordered steak and fries from the hotel dining room. He resolved the problem of where the boy would stay by calling home and obtaining Miss Charmin's permission to put him up at their place.

They gathered at Shooter's house early the next morning and after breakfast sat at the kitchen table with a tape recorder. Communicating proved more of a problem than anticipated and Shooter called on a friend formerly with the Foreign Officers School at the air base to interpret. They spent the day questioning Juan and learning of his family's wretched lives in the fetters of Twentieth Century human bondage.

Juan's story matched what his sister Cristina told Jasmine. They were small children when the Coyotes brought them to the Gooden estate with their parents from Mexico. From an early age Juan had served as a houseboy at the mansion; his sister worked in the community kitchen or mess hall; and his parents slaved in the fields.

Growing up on the estate was all he knew. He did not attend school and was not allowed off the estate except on rare occasions and then only under the watchful eye of a guard. At first the elderly owners of the estate had treated his family and the other laborers with benign servitude. Their concern was for cheap labor; hired overseers, some white and some of Mexican descent, managed the labor force. The laborers' lives changed dramatically with the death of the Gooden elders in an explosive fire at the mansion. The transition turned life in the fields to one of misery, fear and even death within the growing labor force.

When asked who was in charge since the owners died in the fire, fear and loathing showed in the boy's eyes. He pulled his shirt up over his back and revealed deep whelps from beatings inflicted on him by their grandson Junior who became heir to the estate. Life grew even more unbearable with the arrival of a man with a scarred face and glass eye who was known to the laborers as Mighty Whitey among other names. It was rumored that he had been in prison for killing a man. There was talk that he was Junior's real father, although they had no evidence.

Did others die in the fire he was asked? A young man and woman perished, he said. He assumed they were family but he didn't know their relationship. There could have been others, he didn't know. They had a child, a daughter, who was said to have survived the fire but no longer lived at the estate. He had no knowledge of what happened to the child. He understood that the elderly couple's grandson Junior was the only adult survivor.

Falcon showed him the flyer with M's daughter's picture. He positively identified her as the young woman whose body was burned beyond recognition in the mansion fire. When reminded that his sister Cristina had not been able to identify the woman on the flyer, he explained that she lived in the labor camp with her parents and unlike him she did not have access to the family in the mansion.

When asked if someone deliberately set the fire or was it an ac-cident, the boy could not speak with certainty. He acknowledged there were rumors of arson, mostly whispers among the laborers who were too fearful to voice their suspicions aloud and no charges were ever brought. If the fire was deliberately set the laborers knew the finger of suspicion would be pointed at one of them—therein the guile of subjugation.

What crops were grown on the estate, he was asked? To the best of his knowledge the Gooden family had grown food crops but since their deaths Junior and the man called Mighty Whitey had become drug lords. They had connections with the Mexican cartels and were now running a massive drug operation. The only crops were marijuana and poppy plants. The laborers operated methamphetamine labs as well. There was a landing strip on the estate and the Coyotes used small planes and trucks to smuggle in slave labor and heroin.

What about the mining activities and the hunting club? There was no mining that the boy knew about. That could only be a cover for the loud explosions and weapons fire coming from the estate. He denied the existence of a hunting club as well. This was likely a ruse to hide the fact that Mighty Whitey had organized a small army of white supremacists who conducted training at a firing range on the estate. The only hunting the boy was aware of was when the snipers or hunting parties chased down unarmed laborers or suspected enemies and shot them on the run. They called it good practice for the war that lay ahead, the boy said.

Juan claimed the new masters of the estate and their minions talked freely around him believing he did not understand a word they said and if he did he would never live to repeat it. He had witnessed things no young eyes should have to see—cold blooded murder committed by Mighty Whitey and his army of followers, for instance. He knew none of the victim's names but when Falcon described the missing broker Sam Reuben, Juan said that was one of the murdered men.

He overheard Reuben and Mighty Whitey arguing violently and picked up later Reuben was trying to shake him down to keep from spilling the truth to some woman from the past who had come to see him. Reuben's demise was burned into the boy's memory because of the violent way he died. Mighty Whitey's heavy weapons had used the victim's car for target practice with him hog-tied and locked inside the trunk.

Juan's lack of education and pidgin speech kept him from grasping all that transpired between the two men but he understood enough to know the woman in their conversation (presumed to be M) was in grave danger. He also overheard a threat about silencing a nosy private detective who tried to extort money from the estate. There was a hit list Juan wasn't privy to. Falcon figured his name would be on it, but how far down on the list?

When they finished taping the interview Falcon had copies made for Patterson and Earl Birdsong. Shooter took Juan shopping for clothes while Falcon went over the evidence with Birdsong in his office. He had talked with Patterson by phone at the Waldorf Astoria and Patterson agreed he should work through law enforcement channels to urge the federal authorities to move against the criminal activity at the estate. If that didn't work Falcon would call him back and they would discuss other courses of action. Patterson wanted to be kept informed every step of the way.

The tapes were a godsend to Birdsong's office. If the boy's story held up it would solve the mystery of what happened to Sam Reuben and was strong circumstantial evidence about who murdered M and why. Beyond those two cases the private eye's drowning in the Chattahoochee was someone else's problem and the other alleged crimes at the estate broke state and federal laws and were outside Birdsong's jurisdiction.

Everything about Catawba County flouted the law and Birdsong agreed that the alleged drug operations, the human trafficking and

other crimes committed by the self-styled army of white supremacists and the drug cartel demanded urgent intervention. It called
for drastic corrective measures akin to the Phenix City cleanup of
the 1950s. So he queried the Justice Department and once again
was given the runaround.

The hearsay evidence of an undocumented, underage alien in
the United States illegally was no different than Birdsong's earlier
unsubstantiated claims, he was told. The alleged criminal activity
cut a wide swath across agencies within the Justice Department and
it would take time to gather hard evidence that would stand up
in court. He was dissuaded from bothering them again unless or
until he had such evidence or came up with more reliable sources.
In short he was told to butt out.

Birdsong then ran the boy's allegations by the state attorney
general's office and got a similar response. The boy has a vivid imagination, he was told, and how could he know in such detail what
went on at the Gooden estate? The attorney general had received
complaints about Catawba County before and they turned out to
be back-fence gossip. To take on an entire county would require
declaring martial law and that was a measure of last resort rarely
taken by state governors. Give us more proof, they said.

Falcon talked to Patterson about their next move. From his
suite at the Waldorf Astoria the former governor too had made
discreet inquiries and believed he was being stonewalled by the
agencies involved. They simply were not going to act on the word
of a runaway teenager.

Patterson was slow to concur in a proposal by Falcon to overfly
the estate and take aerial pictures, and then only after receiving
assurances that Falcon would take extraordinary precautions to
avoid harm or exposure. There could be no doubt about Falcon
operating on his own initiative and not as an agent or extension
of law enforcement. Any actions he took that were in violation

of federal or state statutes ran the risk of having evidence thrown out by the court as "fruit of the poisonous tree."

He further cautioned that the Mexican boy's life could be in grave danger and effective measures had to be taken to protect him. Patterson had the impression that someone in a position of authority, a Mister Big if you would, was pushing back against federal intervention. By now one-eyed Willie Abraham, a.k.a. Mighty Whitey, or whoever was the master criminal in the case would know or suspect that the boy was in their custody. The lives of the boy's family, and especially his sister Cristina, were at risk and urgent yet prudent action was required.

19

Falcon lifted off at dawn from Dannelly Field. He had borrowed a camera from a photographer at the base and removed a side window panel on the Cessna to give the lens a better angle and unobstructed view from above. Juan had drawn a crude map of the estate marking the targets Falcon wanted to film. The boy asked to accompany him but it was too dangerous. Falcon was reasonably certain of the boy's safety while he was gone. Earl had posted a guard on him and Shooter was armed and wouldn't let him out of his sight.

Falcon wanted to get in and out of the target area as quickly as possible with the evidence needed to shake the feds and the state investigators out of their plush offices and into the sinister recesses of Catawba County. He followed the main road into the county and turned, skirting the town and Judge Henry's place and coming back low over the estate from the opposite direction. The plan was to avoid watchful eyes on the ground until the last moment and to throw them off concerning the plane's ingress and flight pattern.

He came in over a heavily forested area skimming the treetops and then gaining altitude as he followed Juan's map into the skies above overcast fields. He dropped below the overcast and clearly visible were acres of green foliage the map identified as marijuana crops. The Cessna startled laborers who were already at work in the fields. He made another pass over the crops clicking the camera as he went. He flew higher and snapped pictures of the hovels serving as the laborers' quarters and the buildings housing the meth labs before dropping back down over a valley floor peppered by puffs of smoke and the crackle of small arms fire.

He immediately knew he had made an error. He had brought the Cessna into hostile skies above a well-hidden military training area that was not marked on the map. The valley was an arsenal of ammunition bunkers, armored vehicles, heavy weapons and troops in camouflaged garb scurrying around. Puffs of smoke came from a firing range at the far end of the valley and Falcon flew low over the range and shot film of mangled vehicles used for target practice. Juan knew what he was talking about. Two of the targets Falcon recognized—one was the crumpled shell of a pink Cadillac and the other the twisted hulk of a brightly painted, psychedelic Volkswagen bus.

More puffs of smoke dotted the sky around the Cessna. Too late he realized they were shooting at him. He felt the Cessna jerk and knew he was hit. He fought the vibrating controls as the needles on the Cessna fluctuated wildly, the engine sputtered, and the plane lost power. The sun's glare off the engine's cowling was blinding and he scanned the skyline for a place to bring the plane down. Juan had mentioned a landing strip.

Instinctively Falcon brought the plane's nose up, climbed to what little altitude he could, banked and pulled away toward the open fields at the edge of the woods. He saw the faint imprint of an air strip below as the engine conked out and he glided to a rough landing, jumped from the plane and sprinted for the woods with the camera strap slung over his shoulder. In a panic he forgot to radio the tower at Dannelly Field and raced back to the Cessna to find that a bullet had smashed the equipment.

More panic as a convoy of trucks topped the nearest hill heading his way. He had made up a cover story but it was no protection against a hail of bullets from the lead truck. He ran frantically back into the woods tearing through the underbrush in a direction he hoped would take him to the county road he had passed over earlier. Loud barking from where he entered the woods and he knew they had unleashed the hounds.

He felt as helpless as he had the time in Laos when his parachute was caught in the treetops and the North Vietnamese regulars were beating the jungle below searching for him. Survival training and George Thunder's Army Special Forces saved him that day but would do him no good now. The hounds had his scent and he could neither hide from them nor outrun them.

Gasping for breath he came to a clearing and fell to his knees at the sight of a barbed wire fence, the back of a no-trespassing sign, and the county road straight ahead. He crawled to the fence and rolled under it with the barbed wire ripping his clothes and the hounds nipping at his heels. He hurriedly buried the camera beside a prominent elderberry bush and staggered onto the road and started walking.

Exhausted and disoriented he jumped at the sound of an approaching vehicle, stepped off onto the shoulder, and thumbed a ride when it rounded the curve. His heart dropped when he saw it was one of the sheriff's camouflaged trucks and Sheriff Sparrow was behind the wheel. The truck stopped and Sparrow stepped out with pistols drawn. "Well, look what we've got here. Who would've thought it?"

The sheriff went on to boast that he had bet Judge Mose Henry five dollars the flyboy would be back. And now the judge would be fit to kill. "You'll be going before him in the morning and he will come down hard. One thing that gets under his skin is to lose a bet."

Going on the radio to report he had the prisoner and was bringing him in, Sparrow confiscated Falcon's sidearm, cuffed him, shoved him into the truck and they sped to the county jail with siren screaming and blue lights flashing. A parade of camouflaged trucks fell in behind them. On the way they passed Judge Henry's place and the sheriff hit the horn and waved out the window with a twin-finger victory salute. The judge fired his shotgun in the air and the Dobermans led out a howl. The parade was for him but Falcon was anything but a returning hero.

A night in jail left him battered and bruised. His captors had roughed him up. Every part of his body ached—worst of all a deflated ego. He had screwed up big time. He made an attempt to wash up but the water came out of the faucet in drips and muddier than he was. He had enough forethought to make up a story that he'd radioed the tower at Dannelly Field and they would be searching for him, but the sheriff didn't seem impressed.

For breakfast a deputy brought him a half-thawed Jimmy Dean sausage and biscuit and a lukewarm cup of coffee. He couldn't keep it down and asked to make a phone call. The sheriff obliged by dialing the number for him and handing him the phone. A hollow voice on the other end said, "Sorry this is not a long distance number. Please dial again." He asked the sheriff to redial and was rebuffed. "Forget it, sport. You've had your one call. Wash up and put on your Sunday best. We're going for a ride."

Sparrow escorted him out to the parking lot where he stumbled trying to climb into the truck. The sheriff shoved him against the door and drew one of the pistols from its holster and prodded him with the barrel. "Get in the damned truck. If there's one thing I can't stand it's a liar." On the way to Judge Henry's the sheriff explained that he contacted the tower at Dannelly Field to express concern over Falcon's plane running late. The tower had not heard from the plane and he was told it was too soon to report it missing or to initiate a search. "It's not smart to lie to the law. Judge Henry won't take kindly to that."

Judge Henry and two other men were sitting around a table on the porch finishing up breakfast when they arrived. He didn't recognize the other men and no one bothered to introduce them.

Sheriff Sparrow was obviously on good terms with the men. They high-fived the sheriff and gave Falcon the cold shoulder.

The younger of the two men was in his late twenties or early thirties, maybe older, with a hard slender face and narrow gunfighter eyes. When he finally did look Falcon's way the long thin fingers of one hand were cocked like a pistol and pointed at Falcon's heart. The man wore hand-tooled cowboy boots, designer jeans and a form-fitting denim shirt pulled so tight it had come free at the waist. With his lanky frame stretched full-length he appeared to be sliding down the chair reminiscent of a Salvador Dali painting. His casual manner glossed over the fact that in this group he was the man on horseback—when he pulled the reins even Judge Henry jumped.

The older one had to be a bodyguard or straw boss. His boots were scuffed and the polish had long worn off with barnyard muck and cow dung. His size 48 loose fitting jeans and 4X shirt hung from a full waist and thickset shoulders. His ham-like fists spelled bar room fights and trouble. His face, wrinkled leather from the wind and sun, was badly scarred. He opened and closed his fists as if they were aching to smash something or someone. He was the meanest man at the bar and wanted everybody to know it.

Judge Henry sought to ease the tension. He didn't seem bothered by the flies and gnats buzzing around the food. "Everything's got to eat." He fed the Dobermans pieces of leftover bacon off his plate. They took the bacon gingerly and gently licked the judge's fingers.

Judge Henry called out to Cristina who was standing behind the screen door with the mysterious child from Falcon's previous visits hanging on her skirt. He ordered Cristina to bring the guests breakfast and to keep the girl inside the house. "This is grown-up business, child. There'll be things said your tender ears shouldn't hear." The child did as she was told and then like before she slipped out the back, came around, and crawled under the porch where she wouldn't miss a word.

Other than the soggy sausage and biscuit at the jail Falcon hadn't touched food since downing a light breakfast at a café near Dannelly Field the morning before and he was ravished. As he took a bite Judge Henry put out his hand and stopped him. "We haven't said grace." The judge bowed his head and asked the Lord to bless this fine repast you provided for us. He sat back and watched with amusement as Falcon wolfed down his food. "Chew your food proper, boy. You don't want those grits lying heavy on your gut out there slaving in the hot sun."

Cristina came out to take the empty plates and the judge whipped out his pistol and pounded the table. "This hearing's now in order. Keep your seats and don't interrupt or I'll hold you in contempt." He glared at Falcon. "Son, you disappoint me. I bet good money you were too smart to come back to our county and disrespect our ordnances. Instead you've raised such a ruckus the whole county was out looking for you. What do you have to say in your defense?"

Falcon opened his mouth to speak and the judge shushed him. "That was a mere formality. If I was you I wouldn't open my mouth. It only adds to the charges."

Falcon stammered. "Let me make a phone call and we can work this thing out."

"Your honor, you forgot to say your honor. Now I'm not going to warn you again. Sheriff Sparrow tells me you had your one phone call and that's all you're entitled to."

"What about an attorney?"

"No attorney. This is a bail hearing, not a trial."

Judge Henry brought the palm of his hand down hard against the table. "I'll read you the charges. These are serious offenses. Some would be hanging offenses in Judge Roy Bean's court. You are accused of violating the Gooden estate's air space, taking unlawful pictures, disturbing the livestock, preemptively attacking citizen soldiers who were doing their lawful training, endangering folks and destroying property by crashing your plane trying to escape, and lying to the law. How do you plead?"

"You said this was a bail hearing, your honor."

"It most certainly is. How do you plead?"

"I'm not guilty, your honor."

"Of course you're guilty. It says so right here in the charges. Are you denying doing those things?"

"No your honor, but not the way you put it."

Judge Henry sputtered. His face was apoplectic and Sheriff Sparrow interrupted. "He pleads guilty and throws himself on the mercy of the court, your honor."

"Well that's more like it. You'd make a good country lawyer, sheriff." He squinted and addressed the prisoner. "That was just a formality. This is a bail hearing and you can't make the bail. You're not on trial here. In due time you are entitled to a fair trial but the court docket's full and you'll have to wait your turn. Meanwhile these two fair-minded citizens whose peace and property you saw fit to desecrate have gone your bail. It can take up to a year to get your trial on the docket and the jail's full. So you can pay for your keep and work off your debt to these fine folks by helping out on their farm."

Falcon protested. "But that's not legal!"

"It's legal if I say it's legal."

"What about my Cessna?"

"You should have thought about that before you flew that plane up here and committed those heinous crimes. They can keep it or put it on the auction block over in Atlanta. You may have a Daddy Warbucks behind you in the Capital City but that don't count for squat in Judge Henry's court. I don't want to see you back here until your trial comes up. This hearing is adjourned. Sheriff here's the five dollars you stole off me." He turned to the young man slouching in the chair. "The prisoner's all yours. Keep him humble and see that he goes to church on Sunday."

The young man hadn't spoken until now. "Get on your feet, dirt bag. Who's your daddy now?" He had a tinny, high-pitched voice and a nervous twitching in one eye. He pulled himself up from the chair as the heavier man led Falcon away from the table, then stood and planted his foot in the prisoner's back sending him sprawling, still handcuffed, off the porch. Judge Henry drew a deep breath and winced as they continued beating and kicking their captive across the yard until they loaded him into a polished black Cadillac and drove off down the road.

20

Falcon came to in a dark, dank enclosure. The handcuffs were removed but he was shackled to an iron post. The last thing he remembered was a boom box blasting out a rocka-billy tune and the ham-fisted captor swinging at him just before he blacked out. The younger man was behind the wheel and had made no effort to stop the beatings. Falcon tried with difficulty to sit up. His back and his head throbbed with pain. A thin ray of light shone through a crack in the wall.

All around him the smell of fresh horse or cow manure and urine-soaked silage was overpowering. He sensed movement in the dank enclosure, thinking it was livestock until a man's angry voice cursing in guttural Spanish broke the silence. The man's outburst was answered by a chorus of dissonant voices Falcon took to be Mexican laborers. Falcon spoke a little bedroom Spanish but couldn't understand a word they said.

The heavy double doors to the enclosure swung open and three swarthy figures, two with shotguns cradled in their arms, stood in the doorway. The unarmed man was the one giving orders and he was backed up by a badly scarred pit bull on a leash. The runaway boy Juan had not mentioned a dog fighting ring but the disfigure-ment of the pit bull suggested it was allowed on the estate.

A hush fell over the chattering laborers but a loud disturbance erupted from stalls near them now exposed by the sunlight streaming through the open doors. They were in a stable and the horses appar-ently didn't care for the shared sleeping arrangements anymore than the humans did. "Let the horses out first," the head man ordered.

"They need fresh air. Then the workers—take off the leg irons and get them some feedbags. Be quick about it. The others are already up and out in the fields. Get a move on."

The man came over and nudged Falcon with his boot. "Save the gringo for last. Clean him up good. They want him up in the big house." Falcon watched the two armed men lead the workers out. They were hard cases who would cut a man's head off and hang it on a fence post without giving it a second thought. They treated their indentured countrymen worse than animals. Falcon figured the only thing saving him from another beating or worse, someone of authority had sent for him.

When the men came back for him, he got to his feet by clinging to the post for support. He was too weak to stand alone and after removing the leg irons the men lifted him outside to a concrete slab where they dropped him. The ache in his head wouldn't go away, a sign that he may have suffered a mild concussion. They turned a pressure hose on him while he was still clothed and then had him undress and toss the clothing into a nearby Dumpster. They dressed him in plain loose fitting peasant clothes and slapped a sombrero on his head. The men thought it was hilarious. "Looks like a muchacho but you can't wash the gringo off."

They drove a mile or so in a camouflaged Jeep to the foot of a towering, timbered hillside where they piled out and entered a concealed passageway leading deep inside. They arrived at a large inner chamber of natural tunnels and a rivulet of rippling water pouring from fissures in the rock walls and flowing back into the earth downstream. It was a scene out of Jules Verne's imaginary worlds. A creaky freight elevator badly in need of lubricating carried them to the top.

They exited into a maze of smaller chambers all empty except one. They marched Falcon into the one that was furnished and dropped him into a cane-back straight chair. A tall uniformed figure was seated at the table with his back to them. An aperture with a telescope gave the man a panoramic view of the estate and the outer boundaries. Seated on each side of him were the two men who had taken custody of Falcon at Judge Henry's place and administered the severe beating before dumping him in the barn.

The middle man swiveled around in his chair. He had sharp Dick Tracy features with one good eye, a patch over the other one, a scar extending beneath the patch over the length of his face, a thin goatee and mustache, and skin that was deathly pale. "Welcome to the New Freedom Brigade, Colonel Falcon." The man's voice was guttural and raspy. He laughed at the surprised look on Falcon's face. "Your name and rank were on the papers left in the Cessna. We already had your profile."

Introductions were in order, he said. He gestured toward the younger man to his right. "Let me introduce Johnny Gooden. He prefers to be called Junior. The giant next to him answers to Shorty. Me? I go by One-eyed Willie Abraham and a few other choice names I'm sure. To the Brigade I'm known as Mighty Whitey. But you're not there yet. You can call me Sir or General. Is that understood?"

"I understand."

"Then let's get down to business, Colonel."

"It's your call, General."

"You have something of mine."

"I do?"

"And I want it back."

"Enlighten me, General."

"We're speaking of the boy Juan. You have him. I want him back."

"I don't know what you're talking about."

"Have it your way, Colonel. We have ways of making men talk"

Abraham was making no headway and he changed his approach. Part of his tough veneer was for Junior and Shorty's benefit. He ordered them to go down to the car and wait. He and the Colonel would be down in a minute. The braggart in him wanted to impress Falcon and if possible get him on their side. If not, he had to go. It was as simple as that. But how much did he know and who knew he was there? Abraham launched into a lengthy discourse intended to gain Falcon's confidence and soften him up.

"The boys roughed you up pretty bad. They'll pay for that. I'm not defending them, but you did throw a scare into the camp. They thought you'd declared war on us. Junior was just defending his castle. Shorty was following orders. It was nothing personal. Neither man holds a grudge.

"I brought you up here to see if we could find a way out of this rattlesnake rodeo you got yourself into. Now I know the Army and the warden over at Parchman don't think so but I'm a reasonable man. I can be a man's worst enemy or his best friend. It's entirely up to him.

"You're a patriot. You know how it is. You fought for your country in Nam and you come home and nobody gives a damn. But you stood up. I admire that in a man. I was in Korea and won bushels of medals. Another Audie Murphy they said and they were going to make a movie about me. Then they said I went rogue and they booted me out of the Army. It's an old story.

"Now I have my own army and we're going to take our country back. We're freedom fighters, you understand. We got the army and now we need an air force. You see where I'm going with this? I'll take you on a grand tour around the grounds and you'll see what I mean.

"First you've got to change out of those Mexican pajamas into some fit clothes. Trade that sombrero for a coolie hat and they'd mistake you for the Viet Cong. We'll have you looking like the hero you really are. You're one of us now until I say different. Chew on that as I'm squiring you around."

21

They toured the estate in an olive drab command car with four stars displayed on the front. Shorty was behind the wheel. Junior was riding shotgun. Falcon and his self-appointed four-star host were seated in back sipping Jack Daniels Old No. 7 and smoking Cuban cigars. They both wore custom-made fatigues and Ike jackets with stars on the epaulets ordered from a Chicago military mail order catalog. Falcon's were tailored for his host and were two sizes too large. Abraham reached over and laid his hand cordially on Falcon's shoulder. "See, you didn't have to violate our airspace to look around. All you had to do was ask."

In Falcon's weakened condition the Jack Daniels went down smooth and landed hard on an empty stomach. That and the cigar made his head swim. He declined an offer to refill his cup. "Where was the mansion before it burned down?" he asked.

"You know about the mansion, do you?"

"Judge Henry might've mentioned it."

"You sure you haven't been studying us?"

Falcon could feel the tension. The prolonged silence told him to back off. The host withdrew his hand from Falcon's shoulder, rolled down the window, and flipped the ashes off the cigar and into the draft behind the moving car. "The mansion was before my time. We were just there. The command center stands where the mansion burned down." It was now a hardened bunker, he said, but the estate had been a natural fortress since before the Indians were there. It was honeycombed with caves and underground springs. "The estate is no longer an antebellum relic. It is a military stronghold, impenetrable if I say so myself."

Abraham was a natural tour guide. He loved to talk and knew the history of the grounds. During the Civil War the Confederate Army used it as a hideaway for everything from guns to grits. The Union Army had occupied the land for a time and completely overlooked the treasure hidden there. Or perhaps they believed the Indian legends that the spirits of their ancestors walked in those caves and didn't want to disturb them. Having their hands full with the Johnny Rebs there was no call to stir up the tribes as well.

They motored past vast fields being worked by migrant laborers. Falcon expected to hear a cock-and-bull story to explain away the illegal drug operations but his host surprised him. He raised his arm in a sweeping gesture toward the fields and boasted that the business venture was a stroke of genius, and all to his credit. The entire operation was contracted out to the Mexican cartel and their backers in the United States.

"They lease it, they furnish the labor force, and they launder the gringo dollars. These valleys are a gold mine of weed crops and meth labs. The hard stuff they bring in across the border. They buy protection on their end and the backers furnish it on this end. It is no nickel and dime operation."

Falcon was curious about the size and management of the operation. "Where did you pick up on all this?"

"I got educated behind bars." He claimed that inside the cooler the freedom brigade ran a college of criminal enterprise for inmates who belonged. Some guards also joined the brigade inside and were now serving fulltime at the estate. "We keep a close eye on the turncoats to make sure they aren't working undercover for the man."

Falcon couldn't fathom why Abraham would be treating him like one of the boys. Why was he being brought into their confidence and told all about the criminal enterprise if they intended to keep him alive? Could they really believe he might join the brigade or did the knowledge simply make him a greater liability and they were just stringing him along? It did not make him feel safe, only more expendable. He would have to play along.

They drove around the perimeter past the open field where the Cessna was parked and proceeded toward a military encampment and training facilities at the far end of a large valley. The Cessna remained in the open but was partially concealed by camouflaged netting. "The sheriff's boys are master mechanics. They'll have your toy up and running before the sun goes down."

The military encampment was buzzing with activity. An exercise using live ammunition was underway at the firing range and in the surrounding hills. A couple of Army surplus tanks and light artillery pieces were using mangled and burned-out cars for target practice. "Nothing goes to waste," Abraham said. "When those targets get totally wiped out we dump them in the lake to entertain the fish. Take that brightly colored Volkswagen bus over yonder, the kind the hippies drive, the fish are really going to like that one. It was here when I came. Junior took a strong dislike to it so we decided to use it for target practice."

"What would hippies be doing this far south?"

"Beats me, they're not what you'd call a Southern tradition."

"I thought I saw the shell of a pink Cadillac when I flew over this area."

"The boys finally moved that one yesterday. That piece of junk belonged to a slick yellowbelly who messed with my woman when I was in Korea. It took a long time to get even. He was still in it when our brigade used it for target practice. He locked himself in the trunk somehow. I gave him a choice. He had a chance to out-run the hunting party but he refused. You might say he got dumb, greedy and careless all at the same time."

When they completed the tour Abraham sent Junior and Shorty

to the upper chambers to arrange a meeting of the grand council. Abraham stayed below with Falcon ostensibly to coach him for the meeting. "Colonel, you didn't come here looking for the mansion on the hill. That's just an old Hank Williams tune. Don't take us for fools. That would be your worst mistake. No more lies. You came here trying to get a lead on a young woman about Junior's age. Isn't that so? Well, you won't find that woman here. I was told that a girl like that came snooping around but that was before Junior and I became family again. She was riding in that hippie bus you saw out yonder. But she's not here now."

"Did she die in the mansion fire?"

"You'll have to ask Junior and he won't answer."

"But why did she die?"

"I'm not saying she did. She might've just run away. These weren't her people and her kind wasn't welcome here."

"There's a young child out at Judge Henry's place. What's her story?"

"Judge Henry has no offspring, just Miss Lillie and himself."

"But I saw her with my own eyes. Three times I saw her."

"There is no girl. Are there any more questions?"

"You're a hard man to figure."

"The shrinks in the joint gave up on me."

"How did you get out of the joint? What brought you here?"

"Junior came looking for me."

"He's your son?"

"Junior's one of many around the world. But he's my favorite."

Like father, like son. And to think there were many others like him running loose. Falcon suppressed an urge to try to overpower Abraham and make a run for it. It might be his last chance but the vicious beating and lack of food had sapped his strength.

Abraham spoke for him. "We didn't know how much you knew, but I've got a pretty good picture now. We know you have a powerful ally in your corner. We have friends in high places too. Some are invested heavily in our little enterprise. How else could we stay in business?

How else indeed? Abraham poured another jigger of Jack Daniels and held the bottle out to Falcon. This time he accepted. What did he have to lose other than his freedom or his life?

22

Falcon was left standing outside the meeting room with two armed guards while his fate was being deliberated inside. At one point he was so weak he had trouble standing and the guards held him up. A buzzer sounded and the guards led Falcon into the meeting room. Seated at the table with Abraham, Junior and Shorty was a razor thin half-breed and a barrel-chested Mexican both fitted out in white plantation suits, tailored silk shirts, and boleros. Abraham introduced the large Mexican as Senor Ramirez and the half-breed as Scorpion.

Ramirez in particular stirred Falcon's interest. His face was pockmarked from childhood diseases and badly scarred from bar-room fights. He had part of one ear missing, reminding Falcon of outlaw country singer Johnny Paycheck's rendition of "Colorado Cool-Aid" a tune in which a small Mexican cuts off a big man's ear in an evolving barroom situation. Falcon didn't want to be seen staring at the ear and looked away.

Abraham spoke for the group. He lamented that his business partners were having trouble moving merchandise because someone had been sabotaging their planes and bush pilots were getting hard to find. "These two gentlemen want you to work for them. The job pays well and will keep you alive to fly another day."

"Doing what? I'm not a smuggler."

"Flying is flying. They want you to fly them down to Monterrey and bring back a load of refried beans and tacos and other restaurant supplies. The cargo is for their restaurant chain in Atlanta, Birmingham, Miami and the Big Easy. The sheriff's boys have your

Cessna ready and you'll take off at first light in the morning. Are you in or out?"

"And if I say no?"

"Wrong answer, that's unacceptable."

"How much time do I have to think it over?"

"Time's run out. You either go with them now and get briefed on the mission or you refuse. Either way you're theirs to do with as they see fit. We can't use you here right now. You'd be no good to us in the fields and we have to make a place for you. I should warn you that the last person to cross Senor Ramirez, they found his head being used as shark bait down on the Gulf. They pay top dollar and play for keeps."

"Do I say my goodbyes now?"

"Forget everything you've seen and heard here."

"People know I'm here. They'll ask questions."

"They'll hear the truth. You left and you'll be back."

Senor Ramirez and Scorpion took him in tow and a chauffeur drove them to a cantina in the barrio quarters where the laborers were housed. Abraham's parting words rang hollow. "Don't you go off and be a hero now. Or make like a rabbit either. We got big plans and we want you back in one piece."

Duplicity came as natural to Abraham as death and destruction. He deserved all the accolades of evil that were bestowed on him by wardens and wayfarers alike. Ramirez and Scorpion had their orders. Abraham had issued them in Spanish with Falcon standing a few feet away. Fortunately for Falcon he retained just enough high school Spanish to understand what was said.

"You take care of our pilot friend. Find a little plot out in the desert and make him a permanent resident of old Mexico. Bury him dark and bury him deep. We don't want the coyotes and wolves digging him up. That airplane of his should bring top dollar in your country and pay you for your trouble. The bottom line is neither he nor the Cessna will be coming back."

Falcon had no intention of flying contraband into the country but the instructions Abraham had given Ramirez relieved him of that decision. He had to play the game out with his life hanging in the balance. "Live it up like there's no tomorrow, gringo," Ramirez lifted his glass in a toast. "We'll do the La Cucaracha 'til the last coyote howls."

Falcon refused the tequila. If they were flying out at first light he had to stay sober. He also had to get his strength back and the Mexican food was the real thing. His biggest temptation was to eat too much. For the rest of the afternoon and into the evening he turned down tequila sunrises and uninspired lap dances one after the other. "What's the matter, gringo. You don't like senoritas."

He was relieved when the mariachi band played last call and Ramirez and Scorpion dumped him in a windowless room with a mattress, a chamber pot, a candle and an unframed print of Our Lady of Guadalupe on the wall. He slept soundly past midnight and was awakened by orgiastic disturbances coming from the rooms on either side of him. If he was going to outwit these goons and have a chance of taking them, the more they drank and the less sleep they got was to his advantage.

He tried the door but found it locked and bolted from the outside. He threw himself back onto the mattress and tossed and turned in fitful repose interrupted repeatedly by the raucous activity in adjacent rooms. This must be what they meant by the phrase, the devil's revenge was a night in the Tia Juana jail. But this was just one night and he bled for the poor wretches that lived this fantasy of the American dream each and every night. What must they think of us, he wondered?

23

It was the darkest hour before sunrise when a soldier's prayers beseech divine intervention and the element of surprise has a fair chance of deciding the course of battle. Without warning a tremendous explosion rocked the building and brought it crashing down jarring Falcon off the mattress and onto the cement floor. He rolled around in confusion dodging falling debris and wondering what the hell just happened.

As he fought his way from beneath the rubble the shattered door swung open and flew off its hinges. The shirtless hulk of Senor Ramirez lunged across the room, grabbed him and propelled him through the doorway and out into the frenzied blush of first light. A low and distant rumble grew nearer, bursting forth into endless volleys of small arms and cannon fire, as a roar of engines and crunching steel closed in on the encampment.

A bulldozer or was it a military tank, had ripped through the cinder block structure allowing Senor Ramirez to make a getaway with a dazed Falcon in tow and a confused Scorpion close on their heels. Falcon, half asleep and disoriented, shouted, "Why are we running?" Ramirez bellowed in a drunken stupor, "Revolucion! Revolucion! Run for the plane, gringo, run for the plane."

The slapstick scene was utter confusion. Men, women, and vehicles were stumbling around in all directions. The hills behind them were burning and the training area in the valley below erupted in tracer fire and explosions. A car pulled up alongside them and the Mexican chauffeur shouted, "In the car senores! Live to fight another day!"

Ramirez opened the door on the passenger side and shoved Falcon into the front seat. He came around to the driver's side, dragged the chauffeur from the car, and flung him to the ground. "Back to the barrios you miserable worm and do your duty. Hold the line and fight, fight, fight!" Scorpion stepped over the fallen man and dove into the back seat. Ramirez got behind the wheel and roared off, leaving the startled driver choking in the dust.

They took a shortcut on the perimeter road adjacent to the woods and turned back across the open field to where the Cessna was parked. Screeching to a halt they jumped from the car and scurried to board the plane when the door flew open and there stood Major George Thunder, fitted out in black combat fatigues and Army face paint, with a Colt semi-automatic in each hand pointed at Falcon's captors. "Reach for the sky, boys, or would you prefer the alternative?"

Scorpion pulled a switchblade and lunged at Thunder. Big mistake! He was dead before he hit the ground. Thunder stepped off the plane and over the body of the fallen outlaw without looking down. "I hate it when a good plan goes awry." Ramirez sobered up fast and went meekly when soldiers in a camouflaged Hummer emerged from the woods and took him into custody. "He's all yours, Sergeant. Find him a shirt somewhere. Put him in the lockup with the others and let them fight for the privilege of being first to spill the beans on this army of misfits."

"Let me introduce you to the Alabama Guard's finest," Thunder said to Falcon. "Do you think you can fly this crate out of here? Our business here is done." He and his recon team were sent there to break Falcon free and bring him home safely. The recon team had changed into civilian clothes and was en route to Montgomery where Thunder would rendezvous with them for the drive back to Fort Benning. They were under orders to keep their part in the great Catawba County raid from making the evening news.

When they lifted off from the dirt strip the Cessna was rocked by a thunderous explosion. "What in God's name was that?" Thunder exclaimed. Falcon looked down and saw the top of the so-called Freedom Brigade's command post go up in clouds of fire and smoke. The entire hillside had been rigged with powerful explosives and a string of secondary explosions literally tore the hill asunder.

During the brief flight to Montgomery, Thunder filled Falcon in on the mission to rescue him. He had their mutual friend John Patterson to thank for his rescue, Thunder said. Patterson wasn't even back in town yet. He put the whole operation together and orchestrated it out of his hotel room at the Waldorf Astoria in New York.

There was one stipulation. Patterson's name was not to be mentioned in connection with the raid. Only the governor could declare martial law and he was no longer governor. He insisted on remaining in the background. For all anyone would ever know he had nothing to do with the Catawba County raid. The same went for George Thunder and his recon team.

Patterson had arranged to get Thunder temporarily on orders to the Alabama Guard as an advisor along with his team. They went in ahead with night vision and stealth to pinpoint where Falcon was being held. "We didn't want the Guard to charge in with a direct assault and get you killed. We almost finished you off ourselves." The team located the building where they were holding him and rammed the structure to flush them out.

They were supposed to give the building a jolt, not bring it crashing down, but the driver had never been behind the wheel of a dozer before and things got out of hand. Good thing Thunder had stayed back with the Cessna because he knew Falcon wouldn't leave without it of his own accord. Thunder also foresaw that the captors might attempt to use the plane as a means of escape. "Would you believe the plan actually worked? Experience counts for something but I never discount dumb luck."

Falcon had questions Thunder couldn't answer. How did Patterson know he was in serious trouble? What happened to Cristina? Who was the mystery child at Judge Henry's and what would happen to her? He had these and more questions needing answers. Thunder said those were above his pay grade and Falcon would have to get the answers from the man himself.

When they touched down at Dannelly Field a message from Patterson was waiting at base operations. He and Tina had postponed their trip to Europe and were taking a red-eye flight home. Patterson wanted to meet with the two of them first thing in the morning. Thunder's parting shot as he drove off with his recon team was "Go easy on the sauce. I'll see you at reveille."

Shooter was able to provide some inside information about the raid that saved Falcon's life. Jasmine and Cristina had sounded the initial alarm. Jasmine had slipped Cristina her telephone number when they were in jail together and said to call if she needed help. When Cristina witnessed the men leading Falcon away at Judge Henry's house she knew he was in serious trouble and called Jasmine on the judge's phone the first chance she got.

Jasmine told Cristina to stay off the phone and she would take it from there. She contacted Shooter and he got word to Patterson at the Waldorf Astoria. They were as surprised as anyone else when news about the raid started coming in. The National Guard forces had moved in under the cover of darkness, declared martial law, and put Catawba County under lockdown.

Falcon asked one other favor from Jasmine. He felt certain the child welfare agency would take custody of the young girl at Judge Henry's place. He believed the girl might be M's granddaughter and wanted Jasmine to stand by to meet with the girl and offer her counsel. He put up his hand to block Shooter from pouring another round. Things were coming to a head and their meeting with Patterson in the morning required his full attention.

24

Patterson looked up from the morning paper and laid it aside. "The great Catawba County Raid, I like that. Just checking to make sure our names weren't mentioned. You boys look fit, considering." Putting their heads together they had the inside story on the raid and began to fill in the blanks as they talked. Patterson wanted to hear their exploits and he gave them a comprehensive roundup of the operation from his vantage point.

Patterson had gone into action as soon as Shooter called him at the Waldorf Astoria with the news that Falcon's plane had crash-landed and his life was in danger. The tower at Dannelly Field confirmed that the plane was missing. For Patterson, who was in ex officio status and on his own dime, the time had come to call in old favors and twist a few arms.

He had worked the phones into the late hours convincing state and federal officials that bold action was required immediately to save lives and clean out a rat's nest of white supremacists, drug smugglers, human traffickers and murderers. They were in an election year and the publicity could be a game changer for some and a quagmire for others. Declaring martial law was traditionally a hard sell for its potential to backfire. Patterson pushed hard.

At the same time he picked up from a reliable source that the so-called New Freedom Brigade's competitors were politicking behind the scene for a final solution to their problems with the brigade. He had suspicions this was somehow connected to Falcon's mysterious midnight rendezvous with a member of the crime family at the deserted air strip outside of Montgomery. Far better they stayed out of it. That sort of help was not wanted and would do more harm than good.

The multiagency assault was put together hurriedly but with military precision. Major Thunder and his team went in under the cover of darkness with a single mission—rescue Falcon and get out quickly. Simultaneously, the National Guard forces moved into Catawba County, pronounced martial law, set up headquarters at Judge Henry's and the county jail. They put the county in lockdown and blacked out communications before setting up a perimeter and leading the assault on the Gooden estate and its unready defenders.

The Guardsmen had orders not to fire unless fired upon but were more than happy to oblige when the defenders broke into the armory and started shooting wildly. By sunup it was all over but rounding up the strays. Alabama Highway Patrol cars lined up bumper to bumper around the estate to seal off the perimeter while federal and state officials arrived in time for the photo ops.

It was too early to assess the full impact of the raid but it was clear that the armed stronghold had been caught napping and was now under the control of state and federal officials. From early reports Patterson learned that one-eyed Willie Abraham had been forewarned and sent Junior out to confront the raiding party while he escaped through a passage in one of the caves leading to the outside. Abraham showed no compunction about sacrificing his own son who would have gone down in a hail of bullets if he fired a single shot.

Instead of a fight Junior threw his six guns to the ground, waved a white handkerchief, and fell to his knees in a plea for mercy. He surrendered with nothing more than a whimper and National Guard troops had taken him into custody. At last report Junior was the center of attention and telling all, in a boastful manner, to FBI interrogators. The massive explosion that rocked the estate at the end had been set off by Willie Abraham and was part of his escape plan. Fortunately, the guardsmen had pulled back at that point with Junior in custody and were not in harm's way.

The distraction had allowed Willie Abraham to save his own neck and he was nowhere to be found. They would be digging for months to make sure he wasn't buried by the massive explosion but Patterson doubted they would find a body. "Something tells me we haven't seen the last of the villainous Willie Abraham."

George Thunder had to leave to keep an appointment with the commander at Fort Benning. Patterson looked at Thunder with pride. "Give the general my regards. He won't pin any medals on you but if it's any consolation I talked to him and he knows what a pisser you are. You boys did yourself proud. The raid put an end to human trafficking in our state on a grand scale and was the largest drug bust ever on this side of the border. Unmitigated evil we haven't seen the likes of since the lawless days of Phenix City."

"Good training for me and the boys," Thunder said.

"Next one's on me," Falcon replied.

"We'll do it again sometime."

"Give me a break."

"Before you go," Patterson said, and he broke out the bottle of Hennessy and crystal glasses, a ritual reserved for just such occasions. Thunder didn't have time to do the Hennessy justice so it burned going down and he left in a rush to see the general.

Patterson had Falcon phone Shooter and ask him to come to the office within the hour and to bring Juan with him. When they arrived he expressed his gratitude to them both for their roles in bringing down the evil empire in Catawba County. He explained that Juan and his sister Cristina, as well as other immigrants involved would almost certainly be called as prosecution witnesses in the court trials that lay ahead. He offered assurances that his office would be there for legal advice and to assist with legal problems that might arise.

Patterson insisted on becoming personally engaged in helping Falcon cut through the red tape in settling the legal status of the orphaned girl presently under Judge Henry's care. Falcon had called the child welfare agency and learned that no social worker had been assigned to go check on the girl. If the child was truly M's granddaughter, as Falcon believed, she needed to be with family rather than a foster home. Patterson asked Shooter to see if Jasmine would be willing to care for the child and would go with them to see Judge Henry and bring her back to Montgomery.

The loaner had died on Falcon so they took Patterson's car. He called ahead to make certain Judge Henry and the child were there before they made the drive to Catawba County. The judge was under house arrest until the authorities decided who had jurisdiction and what charges to bring against him. Cristina was there to look after the child. There were so many prisoners the authorities were still deciding who would go where. They filled Kilby prison, the county jail, the federal prison camp at Maxwell Field and were sending some out of state.

Judge Henry was sitting in his rocking chair wearing an ankle bracelet when they arrived. The three Dobermans were penned up in back with the farm animals. Awaiting their arrival the small girl was standing inside the screen door with her few belongings packed in a cardboard box and Cristina by her side. Cristina had even fewer possessions wrapped in a shopping bag. Jasmine took the child in her arms and hugged both the child and Cristina. They walked out to the convertible with Falcon behind them carrying the cardboard box. He came back to join Patterson and the judge.

They sat on the top porch step declining the offer of a chair from Judge Henry. Patterson took a small tape recorder from his briefcase and set it down on the porch between them. In exchange for the judge telling all he knew about the child and the crimes committed at the estate Patterson promised to take his case and to seek clemency for his cooperating with the authorities.

If Judge Henry agreed to the conditions Patterson would defend him against all charges, federal and state. Suspension was the least of his worries but Patterson believed that if he helped authorities and turned state's evidence he might get off without serving a prison sentence. His major threat had been removed. Junior was in custody telling all he knew and one-eyed Willie Abraham was on the run and the subject of an intense manhunt.

"You'd do that for me? And I didn't even vote for you."

"So you got it wrong, can't fault a man for that."

Judge Henry folded his arms and rocked. To no one in particular he asked what might Judge Roy Bean do and what would Miss Lillie say?

They would tell him to follow his conscience, Patterson said, to do the right thing. "We'll tape what you have to say and have a deposition typed up. I will bring the deposition to you personally for you to sign. We'll have them remove that ankle bracelet and release you under your own recognizance until we go to trial. You will be treated with dignity and respect just like Judge Roy Bean."

Patterson turned on the recorder and Judge Henry started talking. This was to be the introduction to the movie they would make about him. He had enough inside knowledge to send Junior and one-eyed Willie Abraham up for life or strapped in the lap of Yellow Mama, the state's notorious electric chair. He rocked slowly choosing his words carefully. First he told how the orphan child came under his and Miss Lillie's care.

The story confirmed what Falcon already knew. M's daughter and the child's father were the ones who died along with Luther and Tallulah Gooden in the mansion fire. At least that's what their son told Judge Henry when he brought the child there. Judge Henry believed it was more likely that the people were murdered and the mansion was set fire to hide the crime. The bodies were burned beyond recognition.

Judge Henry contradicted Willie Abraham's earlier claim to Falcon that he was still locked away in Parchman Prison at the time the mansion burned. According to the judge Junior had gone in search of his real father and paid to get him released on a work detail well before that. Judge Henry believed Abraham was the one who plotted the takeover of the estate and killed the Goodens and the young couple living with them. Junior was not capable of planning and committing the crime on his own.

He confirmed what the runaway boy Juan said about other murders. M was killed because she was a threat and Abraham feared she was close to finding out about the slayings at the estate. He was also responsible for the death of the private detective in Phenix City and the gruesome murders of Sam Reuben and others including Attorney Bill Dollar who was kidnapped in Phenix City and forced to run the gauntlet against a hunting party at the estate.

Judge Henry had no proof of these crimes but said the sheriff had told him about them and other murders and claimed that bodies were buried all over the place. Sheriff Sparrow figured his life wouldn't be worth a plugged nickel if he ever ran afoul of one-eyed Willie Abraham and wanted the judge to know what he knew about the murders. "He saw it as a kind of protection, I reckon."

The judge told a compelling story that corroborated much of the evidence they already had. Patterson rose to leave. "Let's go boys. That will give us plenty to think about on the way home." He said he would be back soon with the deposition for the judge to sign and to check on how he was faring. The judge said not to be concerned about his well-being for he had Miss Lillie and the Dobermans to look after him.

Between Judge Henry's place and town Patterson pulled over to the shoulder and stopped. Falcon had spotted a familiar elderberry bush beside the road and dug out the camera he had buried there days ago when he landed the Cessna and ran from the estate. "A little late for this, but we may need all the evidence we can get."

Patterson stopped at McDonald's to treat the orphan child to her first milkshake. He asked the waitress if she could put a raw egg in his like his father used to do. She had never heard of anyone doing that but it turned out well. The others tried it too. The three in the back seat had already bonded and he knew then that everything would work out fine.

He and Falcon discussed Judge Henry's checkered career. He was known for his quirky rulings and had been disbarred before. Falcon mentioned that he had been to the judge's place on three occasions and had yet to meet Miss Lillie. He wondered if she was confined to her room or was just a recluse. "I thought you knew," Patterson said. "Henry's wife left him when he was suspended the first time. There is no Miss Lillie. She exists only in his imagination."

25

Falcon closed the file on M's daughter with confidence when Patterson informed him that her remains had been positively identified and he had solid forensic evidence she gave birth to the orphan child recovered from Judge Henry. Who fathered the child had yet to be established since the identity of the male companion who died in the fire was unknown. A midwife on the estate who was said to have delivered the child had not come forward. That was a moot point since Patterson's duty to the court was to prove the child was the legal heir to the Gooden estate and custody of the child should go to M's relative Jasmine.

Based on the evidence M was still in Europe when her daughter came south looking for her natural parents. When the daughter couldn't find her birth mother she went in search of her paternal grandparents and ended up at the Gooden estate. Falcon could only surmise that the grandparents had taken their granddaughter in and accepted her as their son's legitimate offspring.

It made sense that the bonds between M's daughter and the aging grandparents would have grown stronger when she bore a child. Junior showed no family resemblance, in looks or in character, and discovering that he was not their legitimate grandson could have been a relief or at least not a disappointing revelation for the grandparents. Before M's daughter's appearance on the scene Junior was the sole living heir to the estate and the revelation would have been a life-changing threat for him.

One-eyed Willie Abraham would have the court believe that he was still in Parchman when his son burned down the mansion and murdered his grandparents and the true granddaughter and heir to the fortune, and the story Juan told supported this. Falcon found it more logical to accept Judge Henry's contradiction of these facts, that Willie Abraham either committed the murders or had them done. Either way the father-son team was guilty of heinous crimes making theirs a capital murder case. More than ancient Indian remains and those of the Gooden family were found entombed on the grounds when the digging began.

Patterson explained how the evidence evolved and convinced the court to rule in their favor. He relied on Junior's boastful confessions to state and federal authorities, Judge Henry's deposition and Falcon's interview with Juan to argue for the bodies on the Gooden estate to be exhumed along with M's remains in Montgomery. DNA fingerprinting had yet to be used in a criminal conviction but Patterson had associates who were working with scientists to get DNA evidence recognized by the courts. They assisted him by taking DNA samples and providing forensic evidence that M's daughter was the Gooden's legal grandchild and had given birth to the mystery child, thus showing a direct line of descent.

Earl Birdsong's office also came up with corroborative physical evidence tying Willie Abraham to M's murder. They had dusted M's apartment for fingerprints and found prints other than M's on the bottle of painkillers but failed to come up with a match from their records or the FBI data base. For reasons unknown to authorities, perhaps by an inside accomplice or when he was erroneously reported killed, Abraham's prints had been moved into a dead file. After hearing Junior's confession on top of what Judge Henry and the former houseboy revealed, Birdsong's office ran the prints down and made the match.

Earl's office had warrants out on Willie Abraham for the murders of M and Reuben but they had to find him first. And when they did they would have to stand in line. The feds and the state had charges against Abraham for multiple crimes and the Phenix City murders were in another jurisdiction. You couldn't turn on the TV set without America's newest most wanted popping up on the screen.

An unsolved mystery was the question of how Willie Abraham managed to get out of prison. Junior confessed that he learned the identity of his real father and had gone to the penitentiary in Mississippi to visit him. Subsequently Abraham obtained a release or made his escape. The prison had no record of him ever being there. The evidence gave new life to rumors of a Mr. Big, someone high up in the chain with that kind of power. If the feds had the answers they weren't sharing.

Sheriff Sparrow and the Freedom Brigade were all behind bars awaiting trials. Judge Henry was spared a prison sentence but had been suspended for life and would not be allowed back on the bench. Patterson was satisfied the court's decision was just. "That should give us a vote of confidence in our legal system. It's far from perfect but it's not broken. That's what this case is all about, doing right by the law and looking out for the children. We have to do better on all counts."

A federal agency had taken charge of the foreign nationals at the estate. With the exception of those serving as witnesses most would be returned to their home country. Cristina and Juan and their parents were allowed to remain in the United States. They were issued green cards when the manager of the Piedmont Hotel hired the brother and sister as assistant bartenders under Shooter and arranged for their parents to be employed at another local business owned by the hotel chain. There was an understanding that Juan and Cristina would take remedial English classes and enroll in school.

Jasmine was awarded custody of M's granddaughter and she was already enrolled in pre-school classes. Patterson was also handling the legal work regarding her inheritance. He discovered that Luther and Tallulah Gooden had started action to change their will leaving their estate to the child's mother which had cost them their lives. The National Park Service had expressed interest in the estate and it could be preserved for future generations. Even so the child stood to inherit a king's ransom.

Falcon wondered if consideration had been given to interring M's remains with those of Johnny Gooden and their daughter on the estate or at another gravesite. "That's a family matter and not our decision to make," Patterson said. "If the family makes that decision we'll do what we can to pave the way for getting it done."

While Falcon was in Patterson's office the secretary came in and said to turn on the TV news. A David Brinkley lookalike had cut in on NBC's local news to announce that America's most wanted one-eyed Willie Abraham had been apprehended at the border. The announcer found it ironic that the master criminal would pay the Coyotes to smuggle him into Mexico only to have them turn him over to the Mexican police at the border. "There's poetic justice for you."

The question now seemed to be would Abraham live long enough to return to prison and if so how long after that? According to the news flash a notorious syndicate enforcer known as the Messenger had already attempted to assassinate Abraham while he was in the hands of the Mexican police. The TV picture of the alleged hit man was grainy but it looked a lot like the elderly man Falcon had met at the deserted air strip outside Montgomery.

Falcon had a sinking feeling that he was not through with the old man or one-eyed Willie Abraham and their paths would cross again. Patterson took note of the somber expression. "Perk up, Colonel, this is a special occasion. You started out to find a missing daughter and rooted out the biggest nest of vipers since the old Sin City days." He broke out the Hennessy and lifted his glass in a toast. "Here's to military gumption and beginner's luck, Colonel. It doesn't get any better than this. It's like Sunday on the farm."